Scorpion Falls

British/Australian writer, illustrator, performer and producer, Martin Chatterton, has been working as a multi-disciplined creative at the highest level in the UK, US and Australia for many years. Recently shortlisted for both the Prime Minister's Literary Awards and the NSW Premier's Literary Awards, Martin works across a wide range of ages, as well as writing crime fiction, screenplays, and producing animated children's content in his role as partner in UK-based media/IP company, Hungry Head Productions.

Also by Martin Chatterton

The Tell
Winter of the White Bear
Middle School: Going Bush (with James Patterson)
Middle School: G'Day America (with James Patterson)
Middle School: Million Dollar Mess Down Under (with James Patterson)
Middle School: Hollywood 101 (with James Patterson)
Middle School: Rafe's Aussie Adventure (with James Patterson)
Dragonville: Dragon of Doom
Mort
Mortified
Mortal Combat
The Brain Finds A Leg
The Brain Full of Holes
Space Pirates From Mars (as illustrator and writer)
Alien Vikings From Venus (as illustrator and writer)
Thimble Monkey Superstar (as illustrator, writer: Jon Blake)
Thimble Holiday Havoc (as illustrator, writer: Jon Blake)
Thimble and the Girl From Mars (as illustrator, writer: Jon Blake)
Football 4 Every 1 (as illustrator, writer: Paul Cookson)
Can of Worms (as illustrator, writer: Paul Cookson)
Fighting Talk (as illustrator, writer: Paul Cookson)
Pig's Ear, Dog's Dinner (as illustrator, writer: Paul Cookson)
Bluenoses (YouTube channel, producer, animator, director)
Winter of the White Bear (animation feature film, writer, co-producer with Blue Zoo Animation UK)

Scorpion Falls

Martin Chatterton

FORD ST

*To all at Moranbah East State School and
Moranbah State High School where this book
began* — MC

First published by Ford Street Publishing, Melbourne,
Victoria, Australia
2 4 6 8 10 9 7 5 3 1

© Martin Chatterton 2022

This publication is copyright. Apart from any use
as permitted under the Copyright Act 1968, no part
may be reproduced by any process without prior written
permission from the publisher. Requests and enquiries
concerning reproduction should be addressed to
Ford Street Publishing Pty Ltd,
162 Hoddle Street, Abbotsford, Vic 3067, Australia
Title: Scorpion Falls / 2022
Text copyright © Martin Chatterton 2022
Cover design Martin Chatterton
Target audience 11+
ISBN: 9781922696090 (paperback)
Ford Street website: www.fordstreetpublishing.com
First published 2022

 A catalogue record for this
book is available from the
National Library of Australia

Printed in Australia by McPherson's Printing Group

One

Not much happens in Scorpion Falls. I mean, there's your regular Saturday night blues outside the pub and drunk stuff and random hooning and suchlike small-town happenings of that nature, but not much else. We sometimes get explosions out of town on account of the mines, and helicopters flying in and out of the Medullo Industries Research Institute, plus major dust storms blowing in from the west a couple of times a year. Last week some old bloke guest at the Iggy — the Iguana Motel, the place I work after school — got all hyper on account of seeing Jimmy Barnes at the servo, but I don't know Jimmy Barnes from a hole in the ground so that didn't get me too excited. What else? Well, the trains clank in and out all day taking coal to Mackay and one of them derailed two years back. No one was killed or badly injured or nothing, so that probably doesn't count for much either.

I s'pose if you're really looking for something that got everyone yakking, there have been a couple of things I can remember. One was the time Slowy

Mountain shredded the bowlo green with a tipper truck. Slowy told Officer Clark it was payback for the club not letting him into Tuesday Thai for wearing boardies. Him being naked while he did it was what made it stand out. Slowy, I mean, not the cop. Now that would be something, right, if it was the other way round?

And eighteen months back a couple of dumb-as-rocks FIFOs — FIFOs being the workers who fly in and fly out of Scorpi — put stockings over their heads and flat out robbed the Post Office. Yeah! Straight up. Middle of the day. The dipsticks grabbed about six hundred bucks from Mrs Fernandez-Hoskins and took some old fart collecting his pension with them in the getaway car as a hostage. Thing is, these two desperadoes were still wearing their Medullo Industries hi-vis vests with their names printed on them in letters so big you could read them from the moon. Plus the numbnuts used the ute they'd rented from Vinny's Vans at the airport as the getaway vehicle. The best bit was that the old fart they'd grabbed, even though he was about two hundred years old, turned out to be a complete martial arts kind of deal and decked them both when they pulled in at the Sixteen Mile Roadhouse out at Waxton.

Kung Fu Grandad drove back into Scorpi with both of the daring robbers trussed up in tarps like a couple of oversized Chiko Rolls. Blew right past me when I was on my way into the motel from school and almost knocked me off my bike. Which is how come I took an interest in the details. I like details. As you'll find out.

But yeah, other than that, like I say, not much happens in Scorpi.

Unless you count all those kids disappearing, hey?

Two

Before I get into all *that* — and believe me there'll be a freaking TONNE of 'that' before we're done — you're probably needing some details about the 'whos' and 'whys' and 'whatnots' of this thing. I'll give it a shot, but I'm just putting it out there. I'm not all that crash-hot at putting my thoughts down like I'm writing an essay or something at school. So this story's gonna jump around a bit.

I'll start with me. My name's Theo. Theo Sumner. I'm fourteen. I live in Scorpion Falls in Queensland and have done all my life. Never been anywhere else. When I say I've never been anywhere else, I don't mean I haven't been overseas lately, or gone snorkelling at the Barrier Reef, or hiked around Sydney (or whatever it is you do in Sydney). What I mean is I've *never* left town, full stop. Not once. I was even born right here at home, not at the hospital out at Bullreedy, which is where most of the people from Scorpi enter the universe.

Okay, that's my name, me age, bit of background info. Um . . . so, yeah, what else do you need to know? I go to Scorpion Falls High because my mum hasn't got enough money to send me east to a fancy boarding school in Brissy. Which is where practically anyone in Scorpi goes if they're within shouting distance of being loaded. Some Scorpi kids go to Our Lady of Sorrows in Waxton, which is like an hour on the bus each way and has a semi-posh uniform, but even that's still too expensive for Mum.

The rest of the kids in Scorpi — the leftovers — take up space at SFH until we leave school and get a job at Medullo's or Maccas or whatnot. Cos Scorpi's got the mines, there's plenty of cash around town but us Sumners don't seem to be able to ever get our mitts on much. Dad worked at Medullo's for a while — a good job too, not underground or scraping coal like most Scorpi jobs, but in the labs over at the fancy Medullo Industries Research Institute. That lasted until I was about eight when he got a new job down in Tassie and just never came back.

So I'm here every night and most weekends working the desk at the Iggy and —

Ping!

Hold that thought. It's a guest. Duty calls, et cetera. I'll tell you about the rest in a second.

Frank Maker, the long-term renter weirdo in Room 42, is opening the door to Reception, and stepping inside. And, just like that, the temperature seems to drop about eighteen degrees.

'Hey,' I say, keeping my head way down, staring

at my phone even though I'm not, y'know, *staring* at my phone. It's just I don't really want to look Frank Maker in the eyes.

Frank Maker's eyes are scary, man. Y'know like those eyes when you see 'em in a movie or something and they're super icy blue, like there's light coming out of 'em, or there's some freaky alien-type vampire colour thing going on? Well, Frank Maker's eyes are that way. I've seen this bloke about a hundred times in the last coupla months and I still couldn't tell you what colour they are (even though I sort of said they were blue back there). But the thing is, the bit you gotta remember is — I swear on my life — *his eyes keep changing*. And I don't mean they look sorta different in different light. I mean they *change*. For real.

Frank Maker is about thirty but could just as easily be fifty. He could be eighty. *I just don't know.* He's not tall but not short either, really. Which sounds kind of off, but this is what I'm trying to convey with some urgency: Frank Maker's neither one thing or another. He's got blondish hair cropped close to his head and he's wearing dark clothes that, without me being able to tell you exactly why, don't seem like clothes I've ever seen anyone else wear. There's nothing funny about them. They could be jeans and a sweatshirt, but the material seems to suck in the light so it's hard to tell exactly what they're made of. I know I'm coming off flaky here but, trust me, I'm a details kind of person. And the key detail about Frank Maker is that it's real hard to remember the details. *Even when he's right there in front of you.* Right now he's carrying a paper bag in one hand.

I keep my head down waiting for Maker to start talking . . . except he doesn't make a sound.

Not. A. Peep.

Now if that happened to you, and an alien-eye type weirdo guy was standing there on the other side of the desk keeping all quiet and still, you'd probably freak right out, right? Natural thing to do.

I don't though.

Not because I'm some kind of hero or anything; it's just I know what Frank's doing. He's waiting me out. Waiting for me to look up. Most people can't stay quiet like this bloke does. For instance, if I don't pay immediate attention to a normal customer, like a grey nomad or something, then they get all hot and bothered and stuff. Start raising their whiny voices and coming out all 'I'll be writing a review' or 'Don't they teach you manners at school?' or some such similar type of nonsense. But not Frank. That one could stay silent forever.

I break first (obviously) and look up. 'Kin I help you?'

I always make my voice extra rural when I'm talking to customers. Keeps 'em off guard, mostly, in case they insult me for being rural and then maybe it turns out I've got issues about it, and maybe I'm sensitive about having those issues, and I end up taking them to court like I heard you can. In other words, I'm playing the embarrassment card. Plus, I 'spose I really *do* have some issues (keep reading) so it's not like I'm making stuff up.

Only Frank Maker isn't having a bar of it.

'I don't know, kid,' he says in that flat kind of voice he's got. 'Haven't decided. It's kind of a strange one.'

He starts looking around the reception area like it's the Sistine Chapel or something.

It's not the Sistine Chapel.

The reception area at the Iggy has your basic country motel kind of décor. Strip light from Bunnings. A rack of tourist information about Scorpion Falls with some ratty leaflets about the Mine Museum. Cheap veneer wall panels (Bunnings again). A rubber plant that's seen better days. A plastic iguana attached to the wall on account of this joint being called, for no good reason I can think of, The Iguana Motel. A pink neon sign in the window which reads *VACANCY*. A daggy, powder blue stringy 'retro' chair no one has ever sat in. The desk I'm behind which has a call bell on it and a fishbowl containing fading business cards from guests. A computer, an old-style phone, a card machine for payments. A takeaway Indian menu taped to the wall. And me. Like I say, not exactly the Sistine Chapel.

'Sure,' says Frank. 'You can help me.' He pauses and does a half-smile. 'Theo.'

I hate the name badge pinned to my shirt. It says

Hi, I'm Theo! printed in Comic Sans font under a smiley face emoji. Kesha Patel, the Iggy's owner, made me wear it — more on Kesha later — because his cousin back in Mumbai had told him it was what motel employees should have pinned to their shirts. I tried to tell Kesha that his cousin had been to the US and the US is (I hear) very different to Australia in terms of the whole cheery name tags on shirts thing. But Kesha wasn't listening so I'm stuck looking like a dill. And with Frank Maker knowing my name.

'Okay,' I say. 'Can. I. Help. You?' I add some extra pauses to show Frank from Room 42 who's the boss. Shake him up a bit.

Frank Maker looks about as shook up as a mountain gorilla staring down a gnat.

'Yes,' he says. 'I found these on my bed when I got back to my room tonight.'

And, just like that, Frank Maker reaches into the paper bag and plops two gooey eyeballs onto the reception desk.

Three

'How'd it go, hun? You're late. I was going to call. I was worried sick.'

Mum doesn't look worried sick.

In fact, she doesn't so much as glance up from the TV when I get home. She's on the couch. No surprise there because Mum's always on the couch. It's hard to tell sometimes where Mum ends and the couch starts, what with there being so many cardigans and cushions and mags and *stuff*. But I don't blame her for staying on the couch. She has to, pretty much, on account of she's got MS: multiple sclerosis, which she got round about the time Dad split for Tassie. She'd met Dad at the Medullo Industries Research Institute where she was working in the office or something. MS is a pig of a thing. I won't go into it now because it's late and all and, if I'm being honest, I try not to think too much about it because if I do I reckon my brain will, like, EXPLODE or something. My brain quite often feels like it'll explode. And when it doesn't feel like that I usually have a headache. I've been getting a lot of those recently and feel one coming on as soon as Mum opens her mouth again.

'So, what happened? How come you're late? Those Pakis working you too hard again?'

Ah. Okay. Right. Probably a good spot to take a timeout.

There's another thing I probably shoulda mentioned before now. As well as having MS, Mum's developed a bad case of ARS, also known as Advanced Racist Stupidity. I try not to think about *that* too much either. Obviously. On the one hand, well, she's my mum and she's got multiple sclerosis. But on the other hand, she is sometimes totally full-on racist and what makes it worse is she acts like she's never heard of the concept of ARS . . . even though I've told her about five hundred times that it is a real thing no matter how many times *she* says it isn't.

'They're from *India*, Mum. At least Kesha and Mina are. Ari and the rest of the kids are from Port Macquarie. And I keep telling you. They're *Indian*. Not Pakistani. And even if they were from Pakistan, you can't call them what you said.'

'They're from Pakistan. What's wrong with calling them Pakis? We're from Australia and people call us Aussies.'

'Because people from Pakistan don't like it. Big, big difference.'

'I thought you said they were from India?'

I sigh and slump down in the armchair. My racist mum looks across at me. 'Does it look like I care?' she mutters.

'Maybe you should care,' I reply but she doesn't seem to have heard me. Perhaps all this stuff is because of her MS or something. Apologies to anyone with MS out there who isn't racist. I rub the bridge of my nose and feel the first stab of the headache settling into position right behind my eyes.

What with the headache and all, I could do with peace and quiet, but there's a program on TV involving screaming. Lots and lots of very loud screaming and crying and carrying on. It's a cooking show. Mum likes her cooking shows. Doesn't like cooking much but likes the cooking shows. I'd kind of prefer it the other way round but there are a lot of things like that in the world. So it's probably not worth worrying about.

'So?' The ads are on and Mum looks across at me.

I shrug. 'So what?'

'How come you were late?'

I hesitate and then plunge right in like a diver off the top board. 'A guest was complaining.'

Now it's Mum's turn to shrug. 'They're always complaining. That's what you say.'

'This was different.'

'How was it different?'

'This bloke, Frank . . .' I pull out at the last second. 'Nah, doesn't matter.'

'This bloke Frank what? Tell me.'

Here goes. She did ask, right?

'This bloke, Frank Maker from Room 42,

complained because he found some eyeballs on his bed.'

There's a silence before Mum does something so amazing I feel there should be a plaque put up on the wall, or an announcement made by the PM.

She turns the volume down on the TV.

I'm pretty sure it's the first time that's happened since I left primary school. I wasn't even totally sure until now the remote *had* a volume down control.

'What do you mean, "eyeballs"?'

I'd have thought that was self-explanatory. 'Y'know, *eyeball* eyeballs. As in, those things you have in your head that you look through, eyeballs. They were sitting there like we'd put chocolates on his bed, if we was a fancy hotel that did that kind of stuff.'

'How many?'

'How many? What do you mean, "how many"? Two. The usual eyeball amount.'

Mum looks back at the TV and sucks her lower lip thoughtfully. She thinks this expression makes her look smart, like she's some kind of genius TV detective, but it actually makes her look more like a demented duck. Since I don't have a death wish, I don't say that out loud.

'The cops came,' I say. 'Or *a* cop. Tony Clark. I called them because I figured that's what you do when someone finds eyeballs.'

Sidenote: Tony Clark is the same cop who arrested Slowy Mountain, the nudist bowlo vandal I was mentioning earlier. There aren't that many cops in Scorpion Falls so you get to know most of them, at least by sight.

Mum sort of shifts on the couch. 'Tony Clark, hey? Nosy one, that one.'

'He's a cop. That's what they do.'

'What did he say? About the eyeballs?'

'Well, he thought it was unusual. Which is fair enough. It *is* unusual.'

'And what did he do?'

'He thought I'd done it. Put them in the room as a sick joke or something. Mentioned he might be going to have to call in the murder squad, start investigating and all that. Said the eyeballs must have come from somewhere and, since they were no longer connected to a person, it was highly likely the person the eyeballs belonged to wasn't doing so good. Logical.'

Mum isn't looking at the TV now. I've got her full attention. Feels pretty good even with the whole eyeball problem. Maybe I should've got some eyeballs earlier.

'So why aren't you down the station getting interviewed?'

'Because Frank from Room 42 told Tony Clark the eyeballs weren't human. They were from a cow. Or possibly a bull. He said he knew the difference and it seemed to convince Clarky. Although he still thought it was me who put them there.'

Mum laughs. The sort of laugh you do when you're trying to tell someone not to be ridiculous.

'I don't know why you're laughing,' I say. 'I could lose my job.'

'You didn't put them there,' says Mum, waving her hand dismissively. 'I know *that*.'

I felt weirdly insulted, like Mum didn't believe I was brave or clever enough to put eyeballs in a creepy bloke's room. 'How do you know?'

Mum licks her lips. 'Because I did.'

Four

I know you're dying to know the 'whys' and 'wherefores' and 'whatnots' of it all, but I'm gonna put the Mum-planting-eyeballs-at-the-Iggy thing to one side for a bit and jump right to something else. Since I'm not making myself out to be some kind of proper writer, I can do that and, besides, this next bit sort of joins back up with Mum and the eyeballs. It's all *related*. Trust me.

Disappearing kids.

Remember when I mentioned that?

I'm thinking you could be wondering exactly *when* I was going to get around to telling you about that side of this whole mess. So, I'll do that now. And, just like I did back at the start of this (sort of), I'm gonna begin with the first one.

Or the first one I *know* about, anyway. For all I know, kids have been disappearing on a regular basis for years in Scorpion Falls without anyone knowing. But, since everyone in Scorpi knows just about every story no more than six point two seconds after it happens — and I'm no different — I'm gonna assume Coley Briggs disappearing on October the 31st was the first time anyone in Scorpion Falls had ever vanished into thin air.

It was Halloween. I know heaps of people don't like Halloween — think it's a pile of American junk or something — but, being totally honest, in my experience, the people who don't like Halloween are pretty *boring*. You know what I mean: people who look like they've been sucking lemons for about thirty million years.

But when you're *not* like that, when you're a kid, Halloween is *sick*, right? When I was little, I totally got into the whole Halloween thing: dress up at school, trick-or-treat (making sure we avoided the Stubbins' place cos they *really* hated Halloween), lanterns, pumpkins, the whole lot.

So when Coley Briggs disappeared on Halloween it sort of felt *right*. Not right that he vanished, but right it happened on that night of all nights. It was *apt* (look it up).

I know people disappear all the time. Most times though, someone knows where they've gone. Or, at least, have a pretty good idea 'bout where they might've gone. Maybe they got sick, or moved town, or they go and pop up again somewhere else after a while. Even the ones you don't know about you sort of do *know* about. Like the three miners who went missing after the gas explosion in Medullo East Shaft 17. Their bodies never got found, but we all know they're still down there. Or when Kayleen Minto, a Scorpion Falls High Year 12 student, disappeared at the same time as Mr Fuller, the English supply teacher. They showed up in Bali three months later, married, but before they *did* show up, everyone knew they hadn't been abducted by aliens or nothing. They'd just run off together. It was obvious.

And kids had run off too before. Sometimes they never came back, but they always had something about them that told us nothing too weird had happened. They'd gone, had enough. Took off to Brissy or Sydney or some other joint to get away from Scorpi. We got plenty of FIFOs who come and go, and no one gives a rat's about them. No one knows the FIFOs from a hole in the ground. They fly in, they fly out. If one of them disappeared, who would know or care?

But when Coley Briggs vanished it was another kettle of fish altogether.

For one thing, Coley Briggs isn't the kind of kid who you'd think would vanish. No, Coley's the kind of kid you *hope* would vanish. A loudmouth bully from a long line of loudmouth bullies with a tongue on him that he never *ever* hesitates to use. Big unit too; at thirteen he could easily have passed for a full-grown man if it wasn't for his squeaky voice. Yeah, that's a funny thing 'bout ol' Briggsy — not that I ever called him that — he speaks like he's been sucking helium. It's real funny — hysterical, tbh — but you kept that to yourself if you didn't want a bashing which was highly likely around Coley Briggs. Briggs was real keen on bashing as a concept. It was totally one of his favourite things. If it was an Olympic sport, he'd at least be on the Aussie team if not a medallist.

And, fair play to the Briggsmeister, he wasn't a speck shy about handing out bashings. Even with me being almost year older than him he'd bashed me good a coupla times — although that's not that impressive seeing as I'm someone who gets bashed pretty frequently, mainly on account of how I look and how I act and everything I say and do.

Coley Briggs bashed me at school when he said I'd been looking at him funny and he didn't like creeps like me looking at him funny and did I think — *bash* — that was funny? Thing is, I *did* think it was funny, because he was doing all the big talk with that helium voice, so I couldn't help laughing more and that only drove him more crazy and he squeaked more and I laughed more and so it went on. I mean it *hurt* and everything, but Briggs couldn't see why even *that* could be funny: that I was being hurt by someone who sounded like Mickey Mouse. That you could laugh *and* be getting hit at the same time.

Anyway, I'm going off track.

The night Briggs vanishes is Halloween but it's also the night the drought breaks, like proper *breaks*. Scorpi's not a big farmy type place, but we knew we was in a drought all right. I mean, jeez, how could you miss something like that? Maybe if the rain hadn't come, Coley Briggs'd still be running round town bullying away like normal. Who knows? Anyway, although it's Halloween and everything, Briggsy's at footy practice because that's what the SFHS bully brigade *do* on a Wednesday night, Halloween or not. They *live* for it, man. And, cos the rain comes down so hard that night, they cut practice short and send everyone home.

Briggs only lives about a kilometre from the Bill Windlass Oval and walks it with a couple of his sidekicks until they turn off at Yarranabee Road. He starts jogging the last coupla hundred metres, although he must've already been soaked through. The rain's coming down so hard now it turns everything white, almost like a fog, and Coley Briggs can't see ten metres ahead of himself. Angry at being wet, he picks up a stone from the kerb and scrapes it viciously along the doors of a neighbour's car, a Holden, because that's what the Briggses of this world do when they have a problem: they *vent*. Plus, he reckons that as Halloween is Mischief Night or something it's almost like he's got permission.

Briggs is so busy scraping his stupid stone he doesn't notice the guy pull up in the van.

It's the kind of van you don't usually pay much attention to, just your typical white tradie van with no markings like a zillion others. It stops next to Coley, nice and easy, no aggression.

Briggs puts the stone he's used to damage the neighbour's car behind his back and tries to look like someone who hasn't been vandalising a car. I figure he's thinking the bloke in the van might have seen him and be about to dob him in or something.

The guy from the white van walks through the rain towards Coley Briggs and stops. Your classic random creepy stranger on Halloween scenario.

Now, here's the thing.

Coley Briggs isn't some wet-behind-the-ears *victim* type kid who just gets into some random creep's car because the random creep just *wants* him to. Nuh-uh. If the creep tries to drag him inside, I'm fairly confident Coley Briggs would make it very difficult indeed for the creep to make that happen. Not unless the creep has a gun or something and even then Briggsy has the secret stone behind his back. Plus, Coley Briggs is a pretty fast runner who is only about fifty metres from home. If this guy does turn out to be bad then Briggsy is confident he can run off easily.

'You're wet,' the creep in the white van says and, after a brief hesitation, Briggs nods.

'Yeah.'

'Get in,' says the guy.

And Coley Briggs does exactly that without so much as a murmur. *He gets in.*

The white van drives off — no hurry, no screaming tyres or over-revving engine — and fades into the curtains of white rain driving down Yarranabee Road.

At 7.03 pm exactly, Briggs is gone from Scorpion Falls, as quick as you can snap your fingers. As quick as the sun dipping behind the horizon. As quick as insert your own simile, I don't *care*, understand? The Briggster's *gone* and that's all anyone needs to know. All that's left behind is his pathetic secret stone lying on the wet tarmac.

But how do *you* know all of this, I hear you ask?

Well, the fact is, I know all this because I saw the whole thing. I was *there*.

Five

First off, let me get one thing out of the way; I'm not completely sure the weird guy in the white van is or isn't Frank Maker from Room 42.

It would be a totally legit thing for me to think it's Maker because the weird guy in the white van *is* the same *kind* of weird as Frank Maker. The way he sort of moves lightly so you can't hear a step, the way he speaks — *you're wet* — with no accent, the way you can't quite pin down anything about him. And when the guy gets out of the white van I just . . . can't really *see* him too well, which is kind of off because the bloke's right *there*. But there's no getting round this point: even though the guy's right *there*, the fact is, exactly like with Frank from Room 42, I can't seem to focus on any single detail about him. Later, when I'm back behind the desk at the Iggy, I try to remember as much as I can but it's like trying to juggle an eel. Nothing will stick except the basics, and, much to my surprise, the rego number of the white van: M8ER WD10.

So I'm on my way in to work and that route takes

me past the Bill Windlass Oval. Oh yeah, and, while this isn't all that important to the story, I'm dressed as Frankenstein. To be totally accurate, I'm dressed as Frankenstein's *Monster*, Frankenstein being the scientist who created the creature we all think is called Frankenstein. Anyway, whatever, the main point is I'm wearing the costume: rubbery 'big forehead' mask complete with scar and a flat head. I got a trick bolt sticking through my neck. I'm painted kind of pale green and wearing the usual Frankenstein's Monster get up. This is not cos I'm going trick-or-treating; it's because Kesha at the Iggy thought it'd be good if we all dressed up for Halloween. I reckon it was all Ari's idea of a joke to get me wearing the rig going across Scorpi like a freak. So, that's the setup; me as Frankenstein's Monster, plus I'm wet which puts me in no condition to deal with Coley Briggs and two of his sidekicks, Hunter Norman and Bailey Black, who I almost run into when I come round the corner.

Fortunately, the three numbnuts *don't* see me so I get off my bike and hang back a little, staying out of sight. It really wouldn't be a good scene if they saw me dressed like this.

I follow them at a safe distance, not because I want to, but because my route to the Iggy takes me along Yarranabee Road. I know Briggs lives there, so figure I'll get back on my bike once he's safely inside his house. I could just ride past them but Briggs once — for a joke, har har — knocked me off my bike and, man, that hurt like crazy. So I hang back.

Two minutes later, as predicted, Norman and Black peel off from their boss and Coley Briggs turns into Yarranabee Road with me not far behind. About thirty metres down Yarranabee Road, the white van cruises right past me, like real close, so the van guy definitely sees *me* walking along before he ever gets to Briggs. He won't have seen my face cos I'm all sorta hunched up, plus I'm dressed as Frankenstein's Monster but, even so, I'm dead set certain I would've looked a way easier target than Coley Briggs.

But the van doesn't stop at me.

Instead, it drifts past, the tyres whispering wetly. The driver glances my way as he passes. I register that he looks similar to Frank Maker but, like I said, not so much that I'm certain it *is* Frank Maker.

Coley Briggs is a pale shadow up ahead, a grey shape against the white-grey curtain of rain.

It seems to me there's a drop in the noise levels. The rain still sounds like the hiss you get when a tyre deflates, but I can't hear much from the engine of the white van. It's as if the van, Briggs and myself are in a bubble formed by the sheets of rain. The rest of the universe might as well not exist.

A screeching sound cuts through the eerie silence as Briggs scratches the Holden with the stone. The stone against the steel makes a sound that cuts through the rain. It's a horrible sound. The kind of sound I imagine a bone saw makes in an operating theatre. It makes me wince and I close my eyes as though doing *that* would somehow shut out the noise. There's something hovering at the edge of my brain that registers the sound as being important. *Remember this,* I say to myself. I don't know why that might be but there it is: the noise might mean something. I file the observation and try to remember to come back to it later.

The white van comes to a halt and I step behind a nearby tree. I peek round the side and then dart my head back in as the driver of the white van looks directly at me. I'm not certain he's seen me, but he certainly knows I'm back here because he passed me a few seconds ago. He looks at Coley Briggs.

You're wet.

Yeah.

Get in.

And that's it. Coley Briggs gets in the van and it drives through the rain into white nothingness. Briggs is gone.

For a few moments I stay right where I am. It seems safer there and dryer. The rain comes down harder. So hard that it seems to erase everything I've just seen. I can hear the spatter of heavier water drops bouncing off the leaves and I realise that the sound of the world has come back. I let out a long breath.

'Hey,' says a voice behind me. 'Freak boy.'

I play it cool by jumping about three metres in

the air. When I land, my heart is beating much faster than is healthy.

I whirl round to see who it is and when I do, I wish I hadn't.

Standing right there is Coley Briggs.

Six

This cannot be real. I saw Briggs get in the van, saw him with my own eyes. I just saw him.

This. Cannot. Be. Real.

Briggs Mk2 jabs a very real finger into my very real ribs, producing very real pain.

'What are you doing hanging round my street, *weirdo*? You stalking me or something? And why are you dressed like that, you total freak?'

'Why aren't you in the van, Briggs?' I blurt out. I'm still too stunned to think of anything clever or reflect on exactly how wise it is to be questioning someone with Briggs' capacity for violence. I really want to know how the hell Coley Briggs is standing right in front of me in the pouring rain *when I've just seen him being driven away by a creepy guy in a white van.*

Up to this point, Briggs has been looking at me with just his usual level of total contempt and slack-jawed hatred. At my question, his eyes narrow dangerously and he takes a step closer.

'What van, you dipstick?' he growls. Obviously when I say 'he growls' I mean 'he squeaks'. 'And what do you mean, "Why aren't I in it"? What are you *talking* about, weirdo?'

'But I *saw* you,' I insist, still not ready to compute what's happening, *still* not seeing the risk I'm taking disagreeing with a soaking wet and already annoyed Coley Briggs. To be fair, if I was Briggs and someone was telling me I should be in a white van when I'm clearly *not* in a white van, I might get pretty mad too.

Although that doesn't stop me carrying on like a total pork chop.

I point down Yarranabee Road in the direction the white van had gone.

'It went that way!' I yell. 'Even someone as dumb as you musta seen it!' When I turn back to explain I never meant to use the word 'dumb' and would Coley please accept my sincere apologies, the inevitable happens and my face connects with Coley Briggs' fist. Hard.

I land flat on my rear end on the wet grass and Briggs leans over me, his fist still clenched, breathing heavily, his face as red as I've ever seen it before. Which is pretty red, believe me. The guy could do a class impersonation of a beetroot if he needed to. Although why anyone would ever need to impersonate a beetroot is not something I got an answer for. I realise I'm getting off topic and wonder if I'm concussed from Briggsy's punch.

I don't get a chance to figure that out.

'Dog!' Briggs punches me again as the main

course and gives me a kick for dessert. 'Go hang out with your little Asian girlfriend, you gayboy!'

I don't point out the obvious problem in El Briggso's homophobic logic because I'm still dealing with the 'Asian girlfriend' thing. Him talking about Ari in that way makes me so mad I briefly consider punching back before I realise where that would end up. In my case, the hospital. Briggs *really* didn't like me calling him dumb. I rub my leg where his boot had connected and watch Briggs stalk his way to the front gate of his house. He pushes it open and glances back at me in disgust before moving out of my sight. Only when he's gone do I allow my shoulders to sag. I breathe out heavily. My face hurts like crazy but not as bad as it would have done if I hadn't had the rubber Frankenstein's Monster mask on.

Maybe Briggs is right.

Maybe I really am a weirdo. I mean, I saw that white van, saw Briggs get in but then Briggs popped up right next to me so I can't have seen what I know I saw. It's impossible, couldn't have happened. Yet I did see it. It did happen.

I get to my feet, wet, bruised and confused, and pick up my bike. The rain's still bouncing down but it hardly registers. I adjust my Frankenstein headgear mask thing which had been knocked sideways during Briggsy's little tanty.

And that's when I see the dinosaur.

Seven

It's a T-Rex, crossing the top of Yarranabee Road and moving fast towards the Bowling Club. It crosses the street and, turning into the car park, heads directly for the main entrance through the rain, holding a golf umbrella in its right claw.

Pedalling hard, I arrive at the Bowlo carpark just in time to see the T-Rex push open the doors to the building and duck inside. Coming so soon after the two Coley Briggses, I'm starting to seriously doubt my own mental health when a car pulls up and a couple dressed as zombies get out and scurry for the shelter of the club.

Halloween Fancy Dress Kwiz! reads a poster in the window. *Big prizes! Happy Hour Specials!*

Of course. Halloween. And it's Wednesday which means Quiz Night at the Bowlo. Mum loves it when she can come along, usually only when I'm not working. It's not always fancy dress but Terry, the Bowlo bar manager, always tries to increase the numbers of bums on seats whenever there's something about the date he can work on; like Halloween.

Which explains the T-Rex.

I cross that one off my 'things I really need to think about' list. It's not much, but it's a start, and one I'm relieved about as it stops me thinking I've totally lost the plot. Solving the Great Scorpion Falls T-Rex Mystery means I've only got the Coley Briggs Mystery to worry about. Plus Mum's racism and MS, the meaning of life, what Ari really thinks about me, and why cats exist. I mean, seriously, what is the point of cats?

Leaving the Bowlo, I pedal hard through the rain the rest of the way to the Iggy. It may not surprise you to learn that I am the only one in fancy dress. Ari practically spews with laughing so hard when she sees me.

'Thanks,' I say, removing my Frankenstein's Monster headpiece.

'I never thought you'd go for it!' says Ari. 'Not in a million years!'

'You know I cycled across town wearing this getup?'

Ari laughs so much when she hears this, she has to hold up a hand to give herself some recovery time. After a few seconds she breathes again. 'Leave it on. Please, Theo, please, I'm begging you. It really suits you.' And then she starts in again, laughing. I throw the mask at her but it doesn't stop her.

I don't mention Coley Briggs. Don't know why but I don't.

Okay, so that happened 'bout three weeks ago. Now I'm gonna do one of those fast-forwarding things they do in the movies and bring you back in to right now. Which, as I recall, was just as Mum dropped the bombshell that it was *her* who'd put the pair of eyeballs in weirdo Frank Maker's room at the Iggy.

'You put the eyeballs in Room 42?' I look at Mum and sort of shake my head. '*You* did? How? And why?'

I'm not sure which of those questions is more important. I guess all of 'em. And I'm definitely not sure I really want to know the answers. That's my *mum*, bro, who's been creeping around in her wheelchair putting eyeballs in random motel rooms. That's the kind of thing that can give a guy issues. I mean, don't get me wrong, I've *got* issues already, a tonne of 'em, but if I *didn't* this is the kind of mum-based activity which would totally get the ball rolling.

Mum has her attention back on the TV. The cooking show is going *off*.

'Hmm?'

'Explain,' I snap. I turn off the TV to show I mean business. 'From the start. I want the whole bit. When you did it, why you did it and how you did it. And then I want to know what I'm supposed to make of it all. Okay?'

Mum doesn't reply.

'Okay?' I repeat and this time she turns to me.

'Okay, okay,' she says and holds up a hand. 'Jeezus.'

Mum takes a deep breath and scrunches up her eyes. She pinches the bridge of her nose as if she's dredging up some memory too painful to actually talk about.

It's all fake. I'm not buying it. Not for a single solitary second. Mum is just not the kind of person who looks in the rear-view mirror of life. She takes that whole 'what's done is done' kind of thing seriously, so all this 'Please don't ask me to talk about this, Theo' act is not fooling me. I wait for her little pantomime to finish.

'I did it for you,' she says finally.

Of course you did.

I've noticed that as Mum gets older, whenever she has something she doesn't want to tell me, she uses that excuse. That somehow although she's done something wrong, the reason is somehow down to me. I looked it up online once and it's a technique called 'deflection'. Deflection is when you try and pass the blame for something you've done wrong onto someone else. Which, in this case apparently, is me.

'Start with why,' I say.

'That's easy,' she says. 'I wanted to warn him. To send him a message.'

'Send him a message? Couldn't you email him? Or give him a note? Just tell him?'

'I wanted it to be a message he'd remember.'

'What are you? The Mafia? Why did he need to be sent a message?'

Mum stares hard at me. 'Because he's a creep. I don't like creeps being in the place you work. He needs to push off, go back wherever he came from.'

'So you decided to put some eyeballs in his room and let him figure out that means not to be creepy to Theo Sumner in Reception?'

Mum waves her hand at me dismissively. 'You wouldn't understand. You're too young.'

There we go. Didn't think it'd take long for that card to be played. Very useful for adults to be able to use that one, right? But I wasn't letting her off easy, so I carry on like she hasn't spoken.

'Okay, next up: how? How did you put them in the room?'

Mum shrugs. 'That was easy.'

'Not so easy for you, Mum. You're in a wheelchair.'

'I can still *move*, Theo,' Mum says and this time I can see she's genuinely annoyed. Fair enough. I should know better. Just cos Mum's in a chair doesn't mean she's helpless. She can walk without the chair using crutches. Not for long, but she can. 'I got a taxi down to the Iggy and, once I was sure the room was empty, I went in. It wasn't hard. The Iggy's got good disabled access.'

This bit, at least, is true. Kesha and Mina had made sure the Iggy was bang up to date on all that stuff. Ramps, handrails, the whole thing. Ari told me it was only because her parents were mean and didn't want to miss out on any business, but she's their daughter and is always bagging them.

'I got a key from you,' says Mum.

'*Stole* a key from me, you mean.'

'Whatever. Cry me a river, you big sook. And I took a couple of eyeballs I got from the butchers at the Waverly' — quick sidenote: the Waverly is our local neighbourhood shopping centre — 'and, y'know, just *did* it. Spur of the moment thing, see? Didn't mean to *upset* you, Theo. Soz.'

Mum gives me a quick cold fish smile and switches the TV back on. She's giving every indication that, as far as she's concerned, her explanation of The Great Iggy Eyeball Mystery is fine. Nothing to see here. Move on, please.

I sit back and absorb the last few minutes. It all, sort of, kind of, maybe, hangs together, but there's a nagging feeling that I'm still not getting the whole picture. I lean forward and grab the remote and switch the TV off.

'Hey!' says Mum. 'I was watching that!'

'What would you have done if Maker had come back and found you? You'd have been in jail. Or he'd have, I dunno, bashed you up or something.'

'He wouldn't do that! Now give me the remote!'

I take the remote and put it high up on a shelf, way out of Mum's reach.

'Not until you tell me the real story. I'm not buying all this being about giving this bloke some kind of Mafia warning. It's too much effort for you to swipe my keys, get a taxi, find some eyeballs, sneak into Iggy's and all that. It's too personal. Now, if you want the remote, tell me how you know Frank Maker. Really.'

Mum blows out a big sigh and gives me her best hard stare. The kind of stare that translates as, 'Okay, you asked for it'.

'He's my brother,' says Mum. 'Satisfied? Now, give me that remote!'

Eight

'Her brother?'

'That's what she said.'

'So that makes weird Frank Maker in 42 your *uncle*.' Ari raises her perfect eyebrows and whistles. 'Eww, that's some serious family baggage just got dropped on your ass-ets, Sumner.'

Should explain the 'ass-ets' thing.

Ari having strict parents and all, but still wanting to be the right side of cool, changes any word that might be counted as 'sweary' so as not to technically come under the category of 'swearing'. The shiitake mushrooms approach. You get the idea. Of course, the result is that by doing this she ends up absolutely on the *wrong* side of cool. I like it. But then again, I like most things about Ari. Some days, she's the only thing that keeps me going.

We're at the Iggy (where else?) the day after Mum let the brother bomb off. I'm cleaning up after one of the guests dropped a smoothie in the pool. By the way, when I say 'a smoothie' I mean it was an actual smoothie. It's not a euphemism (look that one up like I did).

The pool at the Iggy is the size of the tray on a Holden ute and just about as appealing. The guest who dropped the smoothie in the pool forgot to mention he'd dropped a smoothie in the pool before he checked out that morning. Kesha had been good enough to leave the dirty work to me when I clocked on. Ari's helping me: a job which consists mainly of sitting on the pool wall and watching me scoop bits of banana smoothie into a bucket using the pool net. At least it wasn't a chocolate smoothie. Now that'd be nasty.

For a few moments I scoop and Ari watches in silence. It's nice and, while I'm doing this, I can at least try and forget about everything even if that's just for a little while. I pick up a glob of smoothie and, with a flourish, expertly twist the pool net to deposit the goop in the bin.

'Nice twist, Sumner,' says Ari. We both laugh even though what she says isn't that funny. Or funny at all. Which is maybe what makes it funny.

'I'm an expert,' I say and we laugh some more even though what *I* say isn't funny either. Maybe it's just that when Ari's around things sorta naturally seem funny. I dunno. I just know I like it. When the laughter dries up Ari puts her serious face on.

'Listen, did your mum say anything more about why she'd put the eyeballs in the room?'

'Not really,' I say and drag the net through the pool again. 'She just said it was to warn off the creepy bloke who'd been freaking me out. I didn't buy it and that's when she told me about the brother thing.'

'You don't think it was kind of funny — not *ha-ha* funny, more like weird funny — that she'd gone to the bother of putting the eyeballs there?' Ari's starting to get that look her dad has when he's got an idea in his head: Kesha's one of those guys who never lets something go and I guess Ari's a chip off the old block.

'Maybe you could cut her some slack, Ari. She's in a chair.'

Ari puts her head on one side. 'Hmmm,' she says. 'She is.'

Ari doesn't let Mum get away with much — probably on account of Mum being such a racist and all — and she isn't about to start now. 'That didn't stop her sneaking into 42 and putting the eyeballs there.'

Good point. I keep scooping the pool even though it is now an entirely smoothie-free zone. 'Maybe you should come over and ask her,' I say, but smiling a bit to show there's no problem.

'Yeah,' says Ari. 'I could bring some traditional Pakistani food.'

Ouch.

'I keep telling her,' I say.

Ari waves a hand. 'It's not your fault, Theo.' Ari frowns. 'What made her, y'know, like that?'

'Disabled?'

'No, *racist*, you idiot.'

I shrug. 'I dunno.'

'I mean,' Ari continues, 'was your dad like that?'

'Does it run in the family, you mean? I can't remember Dad much, to be honest. He went before I was old enough to know.'

Ari gets down off the wall. 'It's weird though, isn't it?' she says. 'Her being like that when she's in a wheelchair.'

'No disabled racists?' I say.

'That's not what I'm saying,' says Ari. She stops. 'No, that is what I'm saying, sort of. It doesn't seem to *fit* is what I'm saying. If you're in a wheelchair, then I'd've thought you'd be . . . nicer.'

'I don't think it works that way.'

Now it's Ari's turn to shrug. 'Maybe not,' she says. 'But I still reckon it's weird. It's like she *wants* to keep us at a distance. Like she's got a motive.'

'So she's pretending to be a racist? How does that work?'

Ari steps directly in front of me.

'You've got something you want to tell me, don't you?' I say. 'I can tell when you give me that sympathetic look. And all this stuff about Mum. You're not saying that because you're worried about her. There's something else.'

Ari nods. 'Yeah, there is, Theo.'

'Go on,' I say, part of me knowing I really don't want to hear whatever it is that Ari's about to say. I got enough going on already. But that's not going to stop Ari.

She takes a deep breath. 'Okay, here goes, Theo. I've been thinking about a good time to tell you this and I realised there is no good time. So I'm telling you now. And remember, I'm your friend, okay?'

'Okay. Slightly freaked out, but okay.'

'When your mum put the eyeballs in 42?' says Ari. 'I didn't tell you, but I *saw* her sneaking into Room 42 and then come out again. She was all bundled up in a hoodie and cap, had some sunnies on, the whole thing. She didn't want anyone to know it was her . . . but I recognised her even with all the cap and stuff. I didn't say anything because . . . well, just because. I guess firstly because I didn't want to stir up any trouble for you.'

There was some detail in what Ari just said which didn't quite make sense but I couldn't put my finger on it.

'And what was the second reason?' I say.

Ari takes hold of my hands and looks at me very seriously. Uh-oh.

'Here's the thing, Theo,' she says. 'I had to look closely to make absolutely sure it was your mum because she wasn't in her wheelchair.'

'She doesn't always use it,' I say. 'I mean, it's hard for her when she doesn't and she uses crutches and so on but sometimes she —'

Ari interrupts. 'No, Theo, that's not what I mean.

There was no wheelchair anywhere. She didn't need a wheelchair.'

'Didn't need one?'

'Theo,' says Ari, 'when she came out of Room 42 she *sprinted* away from the Iggy heading towards your place. Like properly running, flat out. No crutches, no chair. She wasn't even limping. I watched her all the way down the highway. She was running like an Olympic champ, Theo. No shiitake mushrooms.'

Nine

Mind. Blown.

But only for a second before I realise the total impossibility of what Ari's just told me. People with MS don't just get up out of their wheelchairs and sprint anywhere.

'It mustn't have been her,' I say.

'Sorry, T,' says Ari. 'It was. She told you she'd put the eyeballs in 42, right?'

Well, yeah. Again, fair point, Ari. 'But that doesn't mean that was her you saw,' I say. And, I think to myself, that's it! There's a simple explanation: the woman Ari saw wasn't my mum at all, it was some random thief who just *happened* to look a bit like my mum.

'It was someone else?' says Ari.

'It had to be,' I say. 'Unless you can explain Mum suddenly regaining the use of her legs?'

'Well,' says Ari and then frowns. 'No. No, I can't explain that. But I did see her, Theo! I really did!'

I sit down on the pool wall. Ari's pretty upset at having to tell me this impossible thing and also because she can see I don't believe what she's telling me. Because it's impossible.

Or maybe not. *I* saw something impossible too when Coley Briggs disappeared and then reappeared, right?

Which reminds me I'd never told Ari that the guy who took Coley Briggs looked very like Frank in 42. And now I'm seeing that I definitely should've done. Apart from anything else, if what I saw happen did happen — and I know it did — then shouldn't I warn Ari the bloke in 42 snatches kids off the streets of Scorpi? It's the kind of information a friend would give another friend, right?

'There's something I've got to tell you too,' I say. 'Happened at Halloween.'

Ari sits down next to me and I tell her everything.

'You sure it was him?'

'No,' I say. 'Not a hundred percent sure. But I know the guy I saw in the white van was the same kind of guy as Frank Maker in 42.'

'Same *kind*?'

'You know what I mean. Hard to describe. Weird eyes. Too quiet . . . like, spooky quiet.'

'I do know what you mean,' says Ari. 'He sort of sneaks up on you when you're not expe—'

Right then, directly across the carpark, the door

to Room 42 opens and Frank Maker steps out. He looks across at the pool area, his expression real calm, like always. I only glance at him but, as soon as I see his eyes, I think — *he knows*. He *knows* Mum has told me about him being her brother, about me being his . . . nephew. Don't ask me how I know he knows. I just do.

Frank Maker locks the door to Room 42 behind him and heads across the carpark in our direction, looking like he wants to talk.

Ari suddenly finds something very interesting to look at on her phone and I start scooping the pool like I'm trying to make the Australian Pool-Scooping Olympic Team. I'm so busy trying to look too busy to talk to anyone, that I don't risk looking up until a minute or two have passed. That should be plenty of time for Frank Maker in 42 to get the message that Ari and I *totally do not want to engage in awkward conversation* and he'll have given up and carried on with whatever spooky business he's doing.

I stop scooping and risk a glance up.

Aaaargh! Bad move.

Uncle Frank's right *there*, just kind of waiting patiently no more than two metres away. He's so quiet I almost fall in the water. I look across at Ari, but she's already dropped down from the wall and is halfway back to the main building like she's suddenly remembered something really important.

Thanks, bro.

'Are you busy?' asks Frank. 'Theo.' He makes my name sound like an insult.

'Uh, um, er. No. Sort of.'

Frank Maker nods as if I'd said something that made actual sense.

'I understand you may have been given some information about me.'

I don't say anything in reply. Is he talking about what I think he's talking about? Is Frank Maker talking about what Mum told me?

'Uh,' is the best I can do.

Frank's eyes widen slightly. 'Because that information, the information I understand you were given, is not accurate. It is from an . . . unreliable source.'

A wave of relief floods over me. The weirdo in Room 42 isn't my uncle! Result! And that's followed by another thought: Why would Mum *tell* me this bloke is my uncle if he isn't?

'I figured it was unlikely,' I say.

'Why?' says Frank Maker.

'Well, cos you've been in town a few months and never said anything.'

Frank Maker looks at me blankly. 'Said anything about what?'

'That, um, that you were —'

That's when a voice in my head screams — *STOP RIGHT THERE! JUST STOP!*

I've got this all wrong.

Frank Maker from Room 42 isn't talking about the same thing I think he's talking about: namely, being my long-lost freaking uncle. And I was just about to blurt it all out without making sure we were on the same page. Which, clearly, we're not.

'That you were, um, thinking of staying,' I say. 'In Scorpion Falls.' It's the best I can do on short notice. I also turn bright red.

Frank Maker looks at me curiously. 'Now where in the world would you have heard something like that?' he says.

I kind of shrug and shuffle at the same time — a shruffle? — and shoot a hopeful glance in the direction of the main building, beaming frantic thought waves across the carpark. *Ari! Help! Come save me!* Ari doesn't appear. Thanks, Ari.

Frank moves closer and it's a real effort on my part not to take a step backwards. He's about to say something when a car horn sounds from the carpark. Both of us turn round to see a plain white van pull up across from the pool. Frank Maker fixes me with those cold alien-type eyes and pats me softly on the cheek.

'We'll talk later,' he says before turning and getting into the passenger seat of the white van. The van turns in a circle and heads out of the Iggy. Showing superhuman strength, I somehow manage to avoid puking into the pool.

Ten

More things keep happening. Things that quickly push the encounter with Maker into a corner marked 'stuff I'll deal with later'. Things like Lani Lanchester. The day after Ari told me about seeing Mum running away from the Iggy — the day I almost spilled my dumb guts to Frank about him being/not being my uncle — is the day Lani Lanchester goes missing.

It happens at school in between the second and third classes but, before I get into all that, let me backtrack a little. After the incident with Frank at the pool, I got my act together and went back to work. I was kind of hoping Ari'd come and ask how weird it was — answer: *very* weird — but once I was back behind the desk at Reception she didn't show. Ari and I had shared a lot of info in one way and another, what with her story about Mum and mine about Coley Briggs, so maybe she was just letting things settle a bit. I'm guessing too that her not appearing might have had a lot to do with her dad because when Kesha came into Reception, he was a bit off. Nothing too obvious, but I could tell he was being all protective Daddy Bear on Ari's behalf. I wanted to tell him maybe it shouldn't be *me* he was worrying about.

But I didn't. Instead I answered his questions about the guests and left, as usual, around eight. I knew I'd see Ari at school so it wasn't a big deal . . . but not seeing her meant I went into school without having been able to talk to anyone about the encounter with Maker. That left me a bit shaky and what happens with Lani Lanchester doesn't help one little bit.

I don't really know Lani Lanchester well. In fact, I don't really know Lani Lanchester at *all*. She's a dark-haired girl a year ahead of me and kind of pretty but maybe a bit of a loner. Every time I see her, she's on her own, but then the same usually applies to me. I'm in Year 8 and she's Year 9 so therefore, to her, I am completely invisible. I don't mean Lani Lanchester doesn't *like* me. Lani Lanchester doesn't know I *exist*. It's not personal. You know how it is. Most of the kids in *my* year pretend not to know me, so Lani blanking me from the heights of Year 9 isn't exactly front-page news.

Anyway, like I say, it's between second and third lessons when it happens. A Friday, which should be one of my favourite days but is actually my least favourite day, mainly because most of the subjects I hate, like maths and history and sport, are all bunched together in one lousy pile of misery and boredom. Not my favourite. To make it worse, Coley

Briggs Mk2 (I'm still half-thinking the original Coley Briggs disappeared in the white van on Yarranabee Road three weeks ago) chooses today to pick on me again. Not bad, just some name-calling and a couple of shoulder barges in the corridor, that kind of thing. Briggs is still carrying a grudge for me calling him dumb.

So I'm dragging my feet on my way to history with Mrs Rumbass (yeah, I know) to try and get there as close to the cut-off point as possible. I even consider wagging school for the rest of the day but Mum's already given me an earful about that, so I resist the temptation.

By the time I make the long hike through the crowded corridors from R62 (maths) to R07 (history), just about everyone else has found their class. Doors are closing, chatter gets quiet, teachers begin gearing up the megaphone mouths — *Settle down! Books out! Page 43: algebraic equations* — when I come round the corner of the block housing R07. The place is quiet when I see Lani Lanchester up ahead fiddling with the door to her locker. She doesn't see me until I've walked about ten paces and, when she does register, she immediately turns back to the locker. Before Lani can so much as blink — *bam!* — the door to a maintenance cupboard right next to her locker opens, and a hand shoots out and drags her inside.

The whole thing takes less than two seconds. Lani Lanchester doesn't even have time to scream.

After a split-second hesitation — *did I really see what I thought I saw?* — I jerk into action and sprint the twenty metres to the maintenance cupboard. When I get there I, I . . . well, to be honest with you, I sort of *stand there* pathetically. I wish I was more of the 'spring into action' type but I'm just not made that way. Now I've actually reached the maintenance door I just don't know exactly what to do. A yellow metal sign on the door reads 'School Staff Only. No Student Admittance'. Someone's taken a sharpie and crossed out the 'No' and the 'ent' in 'Student'. I don't know why I remember that detail but I do. Unlike remembering the rego on the white van that took/didn't take Coley Briggs, I'm pretty sure this bit of graffiti isn't important in any way. In fact I'm only thinking about stupid stuff like that because *I don't know what to do next.*

What I *should* be doing is something to help Lani Lanchester. Right now. Whoever — *whatever* — it was who'd pulled her in isn't messing around. Probably.

'Hey!' I shout and listen for a reply.

There isn't one. Not a sound. The cupboard is as quiet as the grave — no, don't think like that! Jeez, man, *do something!*

I look up and down the corridor. The school is silent. I'm already late for history, but Rumbass will have to wait while I get killed investigating the Mystery of the Maintenance Cupboard.

Feeling more like a total loser with every wasted second that passes by, I press my ear to the door.

All I can hear is a sort of metallic clanking sound coming from inside which reminds me of the noise a woodchipper makes. Wait a minute... a *woodchipper!!!!*

You gotta do something right now, Sumner, you absolute yellow-bellied tool!

Trembling like an English batsman at the Gabba, I put my hand out to the handle and turn. The door opens easily and, before I've had a real chance to think this through, I jump inside and go into an attacking karate stance, my hands held straight, elbows bent, ready for anything. I hope I look like a total badass, but the only problem with that is absolutely everything I know about karate, I got from watching TV. I probably look like a scared chook which is probably closer to the truth. Standing in that fake karate pose I discover something: it's totally possible to feel terrified and foolish at the exact same time.

It's pitch-black in the maintenance cupboard (of course) but the good news is the overhead light is on one of those sensors that triggers once the door opens. The bad news is that the fluoro strip light flickers into life like a geriatric zombie, offering me brightly lit and super scary snapshots of the inside of the maintenance cupboard before, *finally*, the thing stays on. I admit, I wasn't totally expecting it to be so massively scary dark in there and, although it's not something I'm proud to say, if I'd known that fact beforehand, it's pretty likely I'd have left Lani Lanchester while I ran for help.

Now the lights *are* on, the space just seems like any regular maintenance cupboard and my heart rate gets back down to a more manageable six thousand beats per minute. I swear I can hear one of those heart monitor things you get in hospital operating theatres but maybe it's just my imagination going wild. Imaginary or not, I'm glad to hear the heart beeps slowing down.

The cupboard is maybe four metres deep by three metres wide and smells strongly of chemicals. The clanking noise is coming from some kind of cylindrical gizmo in one corner which has a heap of pipes going in and coming out. Could be something to do with heating? Aircon? Something like that — *it doesn't matter, not important right now, concentrate!* But, whatever it is, it's *not* a woodchipper and that makes me almost sick with relief. There is a stack of shelves on one side crammed with a heap of cleaning garbage. Bottles of gunk. I don't know what they are, I'm not a school cleaner. On the other side are two of those machines that wax wooden floors; a bit like vacuum cleaners but with round metal bases covered in soft orange cloth. The kind of thing you'd expect in a room like this. On the wall directly facing me some chairs are stacked in piles. Basically, your standard school maintenance cupboard. Only two things are missing.

Lani Lanchester and the psycho killer.

Eleven

She's *gotta* be in here somewhere. I lift up a stack of paper towels on the shelf, like Lani'd be hiding under them or something. I can only put this down to sheer panic which, believe me, is coming off me in waves big enough to surf. There's no getting round it: impossible though it might be, the maintenance cupboard contains absolutely zero Lani Lanchesters and a similar number of psychos/zombies/whatever-it-was-that-had-dragged-her-inside.

'Lani?' I say in a voice so timid I embarrass myself and I'm the only one in the room. 'Hello?'

Nothing.

I turn to leave but, with a superhuman effort, force myself to stop. *C'mon, man,* I say to myself, *this can't be happening.* I totally saw Lani get dragged in here and she definitely didn't come out, so logically that means she's still in here.

As logical as Coley Briggs, hey? says the Sneaky Voice in my head who now seems to be having a bit of discussion with my Logical Voice. I sit back for a minute and let 'em punch it out. For a while Sneaky

Voice looks like he's got the upper hand — which suits me fine as I'm guessing Sneaky Voice is suggesting we retreat real quick from the maintenance cupboard — but Logical Voice wins. Calling on reserves of bravery this committed coward didn't know he had, I grit my teeth and search the cupboard millimetre by millimetre. Ignoring how dumb I feel (and how terrified, let's be honest), I lift up every bottle of gunk, every box of paper towels, peer behind the chairs, tap the metallic cylinder and even check it's sealed tightly (it is). Next — and I really feel like a total dill doing this — I tap my knuckles all over the walls to see if there's some kind of secret door or something. If there is, I can't find it. And, besides, how exactly do you tell there's a secret door just by tapping with your knuckles? I don't know, but I saw it in a movie once and it seemed to work then. Unfortunately, it doesn't work in real life.

I get a chair and do the same with the ceiling. Now that I've gotten over the worst of the horror movie re-runs spooling through my mind, I give the search everything. I lift each polystyrene ceiling tile but the only thing I find in the crawl space is some air ducting, and a heap of electrical cables and pipes capped with a solid concrete ceiling. There's no room in there for Lani, let alone a psycho killer. It's absolutely filthy too and I get covered in dirt and dust and grease and cobwebs . . . but I make sure I don't miss anything. I might be scared, but I don't like it when things don't make sense.

After about fifteen minutes I give up and sit down to try and think. Which is when two things happen at almost exactly the same time.

The lights go out.

And the door to the maintenance cupboard opens.

Twelve

'I didn't know he had a heart condition!' I say, but Principal Kenwright, the head of Scorpion Falls High, isn't listening.

'If this was some sort of practical joke and Mr Weller doesn't recover fully, there'll be absolute hell to pay, Sumner,' he barks. 'What on earth were you thinking sitting in there in the pitch dark? Waiting for him? You are one sick puppy!'

Kenwright is pacing backwards and forwards in his office. I'm sitting with my arms folded in a chair facing his desk. Kenwright's behind me which is kind of making me even more nervous.

'First off, I wasn't *waiting* for Mr Weller,' I say. 'And the light just *went* out. They do that, lights inside the cupboards, y'know? It was just bad timing, sir. I was sitting down, having a bit of a think and Mr Weller came in.'

'And had a heart attack!'

'I was only sitting there, sir! I didn't, like, shout at him or anything! And if he's going to have a heart attack any time he goes in the maintenance cupboard, well, maybe he shouldn't be a caretaker?'

Kenwright stops pacing and looks at me in total disgust. He points at a mirror off to one side of the room. 'Have you seen what you look like, Sumner?'

I look in the mirror and get a jolt. There must've been more dirt in that ceiling crawl space than I imagined because my face is absolutely covered in dirty dust smears and all kinds of junk. I have to admit I do look flat out terrifying.

'It's no wonder he passed out, is it, Sumner?'

'How is Mr Weller?' I ask in a low voice.

Principal Kenwright sits down across the desk. 'I don't know,' he says, looking tired. 'I asked them to let me know the minute they have any news.'

We sit in silence for a few seconds.

'You want to tell me why you were in there?' says Principal Kenwright. 'The real story, this time.'

'Again?'

'If you don't mind, Mr Sumner.'

I sigh. 'I was coming down the corridor to go to Mrs Rumbass's History class. And I saw Lani —'

Principal Kenwright bristles. 'I'm not kidding around, Sumner! I said the real story this time!'

'This is the real story, sir!' I say. 'I keep telling you! I came down the corridor and saw Lani Lanchester get dragged inside the maintenance cupboard!'

'By a psycho killer,' says Principal Kenwright. 'Or a zombie. Or a bogeyman.'

'That's right, sir.'

'And then you heard the woodchipper noise from inside and thought something terrible was happening to poor little Lani Lanchester?'

'Yes. Just like I already told you! Sir, I don't know why you don't believe me! And I can't help thinking we're wasting time talking in here when Lani could be in deep — in deep trouble! Sir.'

Principal Kenwright leans forward and puts his hands together. He rests his chin on the top of them and looks at me sadly and very seriously.

'We're not looking for Lani Lanchester, Sumner, for one very good reason.'

Now it's my time to lean forward. At last, some proper information. We've been wasting time in this crummy office while poor Lani is out there somewhere holding out for a hero.

'We're not looking for Lani Lanchester,' says Principal Kenwright, looking at me in the same way I used to look at Nanny Sumner towards the end when she'd lost most of her marbles, 'because there *is* no student called Lani Lanchester at Scorpion Falls High School.'

Thirteen

'Do you have anything to say about that, Theo?'

Principal Kenwright's stopped calling me 'Sumner' and switched to 'Theo'. That's a worry. The second thought is: *He thinks I'm a loser.* And the third thought is: He's right, *I am a loser.*

That last outcome has got be at least a serious possibility. First Coley Briggs and now the non-existent Lani Lanchester.

'Well, Theo?' says Kenwright but, before I can reply, his phone rings. Which is good news for me because I don't have anything to say that makes sense. I'm too confused, too freaked out, to get my thoughts in any kind of order.

Across the desk Kenwright's doing a lot of 'ah-hah'ing and 'uh-huh'ing. 'Yes, thank you,' he says as he finishes, 'that is very good news.'

Kenwright puts down the phone and turns to me. 'Fortunately for you, Theo, Mr Weller is making a good recovery. The hospital tells me he didn't have a heart attack. When he saw you he simply passed out.'

I know why. Anyone would've, after seeing me lit up by the flickering flouro strip like some Halloween nightmare. I glance again at the mirror to my right and almost pass out myself.

Kenwright fixes me again with his 'kindly but stern' look; the kind of look I get from Mum when I've done something real bad. 'So back to this business of the mysterious Lois Lanwood —'

'Lani Lanchester,' I correct and immediately regret it. Kenwright loses a bit of the 'kindly' and ups the amount of 'stern'.

'It hardly matters, does it, Sumner?'

I've been relegated back to 'Sumner'.

'It hardly matters because she is a figment of your overactive adolescent imagination. Or some wild story you've concocted to cover up whatever it was you were really doing in the maintenance cupboard. Most likely smoking, if I had to take a guess. So, if you don't mind, could you let me know the truth before I get down to the business of what to do with you?'

I'm about to tell Kenwright that it was a joke that got out of hand (since he clearly isn't buying anything about Lani) when I see something behind him that stops me dead. For a moment I sit with my mouth open doing a decent impersonation of a fish out of water.

'But that's —' I begin to say then cut myself off suddenly, aware that I could get into more trouble.

'But that's what?' says Kenwright.

I drop my head. 'Nothing, sir.'

Kenwright lets out a long sigh, drums his fingers on his desk, and lets the silence grow dramatically. 'Very well,' he says, at last. 'Here's what I'm going to do, Mr Sumner. You will be suspended from Scorpion Falls High for one week effective immediately. During that week I suggest you take a long hard look at yourself and this need to invent ridiculous stories. When you return to school there will be no more nonsense from you about missing students and you will stop sitting in dark maintenance cupboards for "a bit of a think". Lastly, and most importantly, you will also write an apology to Mr Weller which you will deliver to him in person when he is recovered and back at school. Is that clear?'

'Sir,' I mutter.

Kenwright waves a dismissive hand. 'Now get out of my sight.'

I get up and move to the door but before I step out I risk one more look back at what I'd seen behind Principal Kenwright.

It's a photograph of the Scorpion Falls High School Year 9, one of a set of framed photos of every year group. In the Year 9 photo there are four rows of students, each row consisting of roughly thirty people. Sitting in the bottom row at the far left is a dark-haired girl with a self-contained expression.

Lani Lanchester.

Fourteen

A couple of times on my way back home after being canned by Kenwright, I'm thinking so much about the photo, I almost don't make it. The first time is right outside the school gates when I step in front of a truck. The tradies inside yell something out of their window about my level of intelligence as they swerve round me and throw a carton of chocolate milk at me for good luck. Five minutes later I again narrowly avoid getting creamed by a Medullo Industries semi-trailer as it makes the turn into Mile Marker Road, the main access point to the CI West Mine and the sprawling CI Research Institute. The semi-trailer driver blasts his horn as I cross the junction without looking, producing roughly the same reaction in me as being dropped while sleeping into a pool filled with ice. I swerve into a roadside ditch and somersault over the handlebars. The driver doesn't bother stopping.

Rubbing my knee, I lean back against the dirt wall of the ditch and watch the semi-trailer's dust as it grinds through the gears on the incline. The semi-trailers have been around my entire life and, like practically everything to do with the mines, have become part of the scenery. Perhaps it's the shock of what's been happening, or maybe it's a side-effect of y'know, me being weird, but I'm starting to see Scorpion Falls differently.

I fish my phone out of my pocket and text Ari.

Need a fava

I don't mention the suspension. Or Lani Lanchester, or anything about the maintenance cupboard, or Principal Kenwright or any of that. It's not the kind of stuff you put in a text.

I kill some time hanging out down near the Oval and get back home around four so Mum won't ask me any weird questions I'd find hard to answer. She'll find out I'm suspended at some point — or, then again, maybe she won't — but I'm not going to give her any help on that score. That kind of information is on a need-to-know basis and right now I need to know Mum *doesn't* know. Besides, Mum and me still gotta have that talk about Uncle Frank. I decide that subject can wait until I deal with the problem right in front of me: the fact I just got suspended for trying to help an imaginary school friend. I don't know exactly what Principal Kenwright is up to, but I know that I'm going to do everything I can to find out.

I duck into the kitchen and Mum shouts out from the living room, 'That you, hon?'

'No, it's Captain America,' I reply and head for my room.

'Okay,' says Mum. 'Good day at school?'

'Ah-huh,' I manage to grunt out which seems to be all she needs. Since Ari gave the info about seeing Mum running away from the Iggy, I've been avoiding her. Mum, I mean, not Ari. I can't quite tell you why that's so but the fact is, that's what's happening. I know Ari's mistaken about Mum, but she was totally convinced she'd seen what she'd seen. After Coley Briggs vanishing and reappearing, I don't really know what to think about the stuff going on in Scorpion Falls. Staying out of Mum's way can't go on forever, I know that, but I haven't got room in my head to confront her with Ari's story. One thing at a time, hey? And, right now, I need to spend some time thinking about what just happened with Lani Lanchester and Principal Kenwright.

After I've taken a shower to get rid of the muck from the maintenance cupboard, I sit on my bed and try to figure out where to start.

It should be easy. A girl disappears from school in the middle of the day and I'm a witness to that disappearance. But when I tell my story, the authorities, in the bulky form of Principal Kenwright, don't believe a word of it. They also go on to spin some weird thing that the kid who disappeared *never actually existed.*

I didn't know Lani Lanchester but I've seen her around the school as long as I've been at Scorpion Falls High. As I rewind the times I can remember seeing her, a clear image of her came through. Long black hair, a serious expression. She sort of walks with her head down and doesn't have many friends. Doesn't, now I came to think about it, have *any* friends.

I lie back, my hands cupped behind my head.

Lani Lanchester doesn't have any friends. That's a thought worth taking for a spin round the block.

A quick reel of images plays: me watching Lani crossing the school yard alone, her books clasped against her like a shield; a lonely-looking Lani coming out of a classroom and scurrying towards the lockers; Lani glancing at me from the window of an empty school bus as I cycle home; Lani eating lunch by herself at a table in the corner of the cafeteria, her back to everyone else.

She was never with anyone. Not once can I remember her talking to another student or even arguing with anyone else. A solitary person. Lonely. *Invisible.* The words are like a slap in the face. I can see Kenwright leaning over — *there is no student called Lani Lanchester at Scorpion Falls High School* — and, for the first time I wonder if he's right. I mean, if no one *sees* you then maybe you *don't* exist. That makes sense, doesn't it? Trees, forests, et cetera. I need to speak to other students and see what they remember about Lani Lanchester.

In the meantime, there's an obvious place I can start digging: the photo. If I can find the photo I saw behind Kenwright online, then that'll at least prove I'm not completely out of it.

I pull up the Scorpion Falls High website which looks like any school website: in other words, absolutely horrible. Who *looks* at this stuff? I wade through all the garbage whoever put this together thought was important and cut right to the photo gallery.

I flick past images of students, of school trips (none of them involving me), of sports events (same) and fundraisers and school performances. Lani doesn't appear in any of them either, but since the same applies to me, I don't attach much importance to that. I get to the year group photos and feel my heart rate quicken. Year 6, Year 7 . . . there! Year 9. I click on the thumbnail and the screen fills with the high-resolution photo I'd seen that afternoon in Principal Kenwright's office. I scroll across to the bottom row at the far left to find Lani Lanchester.

She isn't there.

In her place is Nathan Briggs, Coley Briggs' older brother.

Fifteen

Before my brain shorts out, I figure the best thing to do is write down a recap of the freaky happenings in Scorpi.
1. There's the hard-to-pin-down weird guy in Room 42 at the Iggy.
2. Who is, according to my pretty flaky mum who put some eyeballs in his room, my long-lost Uncle Frank.
3. And who is probably connected to the creepy white van which took part in . . .
4. The Vanishing of Corey Briggs.
5. Then there was The Unvanishing of Corey Briggs.
6. Ari maybe/maybe not seeing Mum running out of 42.
7. The Vanishing of Lani Lanchester.
8. Whatever *that* was that grabbed Lani Lanchester and pulled her into the maintenance cupboard.
9. Principal Kenwright lying about Lani Lanchester not being a student at Scorpion Falls High.

10. Me seeing Lani in the school photo and then Lani mysteriously disappearing from the school photo and being replaced by Nat Briggs.

Once I've completed the list, I feel a little better. It's like I've *done* something about everything without leaving my room. Of course, it's only a feeling. Reality is, I'm no better off than I was *before* I wrote the list.

I check my phone. Time to get to work. I don't think I've ever felt so good about going to work.

I need to speak to Ari.

'Suspended?'

'A week.'

Ari whistles long and low. I know she's thinking about how her folks would react if she was the one who'd been suspended. Kesha and Mina flip out — and I don't mean in a good way — if Ari gets so much as a B grade in anything at school. I'm pretty sure the idea of Ari being suspended from school would cause the Patel parents' heads to spontaneously explode.

'What did your mum say?'

I put down the stack of clean towels I'd been folding in the laundry storage at the Iggy.

Ari, sitting on one of the shelves, her legs swinging in space, watches me work. She plays with a pebble, passing it from hand to hand. I don't think she knows she's doing it: Ari's always fiddling with things. We keep the door to the storage open so Ari can keep an eye out for her parents who are prepping the restaurant. Fridays are usually busy and I'm looking forward to Ari grabbing me a plate of lamb rogan josh later. What with all the Lani stuff, I haven't eaten since brekky.

Ari and me still haven't talked about her telling me about Mum running from Room 42. I think maybe we've sort of silently agreed not to talk about that until sometime in the future. Say around 2056 or something. Compared to the other stuff going on it doesn't seem that important.

I finish stacking the towels.

'Well?' says Ari.

'Mum doesn't know,' I say, heading out of the door and back towards Reception. 'Because I haven't told her.'

I know this kind of thing freaks Ari out. She seems to tell her parents everything. Compared to me anyway. I think it's cos she reckons not telling them Big Stuff — like getting suspended from school — will be worse if they find out later. So you might as well 'fess up straight away.

It's a theory, but I'm gonna stick with my method.

I sit behind the counter and start checking my list. Kesha gives me a stack of stuff to do every time I'm at the Iggy. Ari leans across the counter and starts tapping her pebble against the wood. It's kind of annoying to be honest. Tap tap-tap-tap tap.

'So?' she says.

'So what?'

'You still haven't told me why you got canned. From school.'

I lean forward. 'I saw something, Ari. Something super weird. Weirder than the thing with Coley.'

I've got Ari's full attention now. 'No way!'

'Yes way.' Feeling like I've done this before (probably because I have, when I told Ari about the Coley Briggs thing), I tell her all about Lani Lanchester. I don't leave anything out; Ari gets the whole story from start to finish.

'And then I came right here,' I say.

'Woah!' whispers Ari, shaking her head. 'That is totally massively freaky, bro!'

'Isn't it?' For a few seconds we kind of sit there shaking our heads in wonder at the total and massive freakiness of it all. Then Ari puts up a finger.

'I do have one question, Theo.'

'Okay,' I say.

'Who's this Lani Lanchester chick?'

Sixteen

It turns out Principal Kenwright isn't the only person at Scorpion Falls High who's never heard of Lani Lanchester. There's at least one more and her name is Ari Patel.

'You're joking,' I say. 'Lani. Lani *Lanchester*. *Lani*.'

Ari shakes her head. 'Repeating her name over and over won't make me know who you're talking about. I've never heard of her. Never seen her.'

'She's in Year 9,' I say. 'Maybe that's why.'

'Uh-nuh,' says Ari. 'Sorry, bro, but I know everyone at school. Maybe not by name or y'know, *know* them . . . but I can remember who they are and what they look like. Everyone.'

'You really, really don't know who she is?'

'Really, really, really,' says Ari. 'Sorry, Theo.'

'Hmm,' I say. 'I was sort of hoping you'd be able to figure it all out for me.'

There's something bugging me about Ari's answer — I mean, apart from it meaning I'm probably just confused — but I can't quite work out what it is.

Ari takes a marker pen from the jar on the

countertop and writes something on the pebble she's been playing with. Then she does something unexpected by coming round to my side of the Reception desk and, after a quick look to check the coast is clear, kissing me warmly on the cheek. It's not a proper smooch-type pash, or even close, but it still sends an electric shock straight through me. And makes me completely forget about Lani Lanchester and the maintenance cupboard and what is bugging me about Ari's answer for a few moments.

'We'll figure it out, Theo,' Ari whispers. She slips the pebble into my pocket. 'A good luck charm. Don't look at it until you need to.'

If I was a different person — say if I *wasn't* Theo Sumner, the geeky loner who's never set foot outside Scorpion Falls — I'd have *totally* one thousand percent kissed Ari right back: a proper rock star smacker smooch and everything would be fricken fireworks, fantastic from now until the end of all time.

The problem with that scenario is I *am* Theo Sumner, the geeky loner who's never set foot outside Scorpion Falls, so I don't do zipedee-doo-dah except make like a beetroot and mumble something dumb. Then Ari does an amazing, amazing thing: she kisses me *again*, this time for real. When she's finished, I feel like a different person. I *am* a different person. I feel like I could do anything. I could probably wrestle a lion. No idea why I'd want to do that but if a lion walked into the Iggy right now I would take that sucker down.

'Let's start at the start,' says Ari. She straightens up, all business. Ari Patel — who I now know for deadset certain to be The Greatest Girl Who Ever Walked The Earth — does a quick check to see if Poppa Patel is anywhere around. Kesha and Mina have, I'm sure, a pretty strict policy on their daughter kissing anyone, let alone someone like me. They —

Ari snaps her fingers. 'Hey, dingbat! Concentrate!'

'Sorry?' I say, my mind still somewhere out past Pluto. 'What?'

'The start,' says Ari, 'of all this. We need to take a look at where all this stuff started.'

'Coley Briggs?'

'We're not going to get anything out of Coley Briggs, are we? Except maybe a bashing. Think. Who picked up Briggs?'

'A weird bloke in a white van.'

'A weird bloke in a white van who looked an awful lot like and maybe was . . .'

'. . . Frank from 42!'

Ari pats me on the head like a dog who's learnt a new trick. 'Good boy!' she says. For a moment I think she's going to chuck me a chew treat. 'The next time Frank Maker leaves his room,' says Ari, 'we're going to break into Room 42 and find out what's going on.'

'You sure?' I say. 'You know that's illegal? Kesha and Mina would go nuts if they found out.'

'I don't care!' says Ari. 'We've got to get to the bottom of this.'

'Okay.' I look past Ari and out through the window of the office. 'Now's our chance.'

'What do you mean?'

I point at a white van exiting the carpark. 'Because Frank Maker has left the building.'

Seventeen

'This doesn't feel right, Theo,' whispers Ari. 'At all. I'm beginning to get a real bad feeling about this.'

The two of us are standing outside the door to Room 42 with the motel passkey at the ready, about to swipe the lock to get us inside. And it looks like Ari's had the quickest change of mind in history. You ever find that? Someone saying something all brave and let's-do-this-thing and then when it comes to it, y'know, *doing* the actual thing, they start back-pedalling? Well, that's Ari standing outside 42.

'*Now*, Ari?' I hiss. 'You want to change your mind *now*? What about all that stuff back in the office, the *rah rah rah* about finding out what's really going on?'

'It's all right for *you*!' Ari hisses. '*You* haven't got a dad like mine!'

Ari claps a horrified hand to her mouth, her eyes wide. 'Oh! Oh God! Theo, I'm sorry! I did not mean to say that! It just slipped out! Oh my God I didn't mean that, that, that —'

'That I haven't got a dad, full stop?' I hold out a hand and put it against Ari's cheek. 'It's okay, Ari.

Honestly. I know you didn't mean it.' I swipe the passkey across Room 42's pad and the lock clicks open. 'Besides,' I continue, 'it's too late to turn back now.'

I take Ari's hand and, together, we step inside Room 42.

I don't know exactly what I was expecting. A bomb factory? Unicorns? The meaning of life, the universe and everything?

It's not like we hadn't been in Room 42 plenty of times before. Kesha sometimes gets me to cover if a cleaner is sick or something, and a coupla times I've delivered food to Maker from the restaurant which Kesha and Mina run as a sideline.

Room 42 sits on the corner of the motel. It's got an extra bit of space inside. Sort of makes the room more like a regular living room, with a small couch, an armchair and a coffee table. Everything else is mostly the same as all the other rooms, except Frank Maker keeps this one *real* clean. I'm talking *immaculate*, bro. When the cleaners come in, they don't have to do anything in 42. The bed is crisply made and I know this is something Frank does himself because Rainbow, one of the cleaners at the Iggy, told me. Every morning, no matter what time she arrives, Frank's bed is squared away neat as can be. Washes his own sheets too, Rainbow also told me, which is another piece in the whole freaking jigsaw. Who washes their own sheets in a motel?

Answer: weird guys like Frank Maker who have something to hide.

'What do we do now?' whispers Ari.

It's a good question, like most of Ari's questions. Thing is, cos I'm a boy, I can't just like *admit* that I haven't got a clue, so I pretend I know what I'm doing.

'Looking for weirdness,' I say. 'We'll know when we see it.'

'You look pretty weird,' says Ari. 'Does that count?'

'Hah hah,' I say flatly. 'The Stone Age called; they want their joke back.'

I point to the drawers on either side of the bed. 'See if there's anything in there. I'll take the wardrobe.'

'Okay,' says Ari while I move to the wardrobe.

Before I can open the door, I hear a faint sound way off in the distance. There's something about the noise that stops me dead in my tracks.

'You hear that?'

Ari looks up, her face blank. 'Hear what?'

A few seconds later, the sound comes again. It's a kind of low rumbling but there's something else there too, something *alive*.

Ari nods. 'Yeah, I heard it. Could be a train?'

She's talking about the coal trains which criss-cross Scorpi. They run every few hours from the loading depots at Medullo's, hauling the coal east to Hay Point over by Mackay. Like the grinding gears and airbrakes of the semi-trailers, the rumble from the trains has seeped into Scorpion Falls and my subconscious like wood stain into a gatepost. Although, having said all that, this is not a sound I ever remember registering before now. But what Ari's saying sounds convincing enough. It could be the trains. Maybe.

'Check the windows,' hisses Ari. 'Just in case.'

I dart across to the window and crack open a blind. The Iggy looks just as daggy and boring as it did five minutes ago. More importantly, the carpark contains zero amount of Frank Makers or white vans. Exactly the number I like when it comes to those things.

'Nothin',' I say and turn back to the wardrobe.

Inside are Frank Maker's clothes. Fair enough, I think. What else would you expect?

Three pairs of black-blue jeans. Three black-blue sweatshirts. Three black-blue T-shirts. Three snow-white shirts. A blue-black suit. Three black baseball caps. Neatly stacked underwear and tightly balled black socks. Two belts, two ties. Everything seems well-cared for; not new exactly, but clean and crisp. Not that I'd know, but it's how I'd expect the wardrobe of someone in the military to look. It's an easy wardrobe to search. I pat down the pockets of the clothes, taking extreme care not to leave any traces. I even unroll the socks and spend a lot of time carefully rolling them back up exactly as they were. Frank Maker is the kind of bloke who'd notice. And I'm the kind of bloke who'd stuff something like that up so I take my time.

At the back of the wardrobe a small black backpack hangs on a hook. I step inside to take a closer look. It's darker nearer to the back of the wardrobe and the small sounds Ari makes as she searches the bedside tables fade as I step further in. I take the backpack down and start going through the zippered pockets, feeling partly like a spy and mostly like a burglar. Also: *I'm in Frank Maker's wardrobe!* This phrase keeps repeating in my head over and over. It's not a good feeling.

I hear the rumbling sound again. This time it's louder and much, much clearer.

And it's coming from somewhere directly behind the wardrobe.

Okay, Sumner, I tell myself, be cool. Of course, that's easier said than done. I'm about as cool as a sanga on a grill.

Cautiously — like super *massively* cautiously — and feeling more than a bit stupid, I bend my ear to the plywood and listen. With my ear to the wood, the sound is crystal clear, and I know exactly what's making the noise. Somewhere behind the wardrobe in Room 42 is a very large African lion.

Eighteen

I whip my head back in shock, slamming hard against a shelf, but I don't feel a thing.

A lion? What?

I look over my shoulder through the open wardrobe door, and notice Ari has moved to the other side of the bed. If she heard the lion she's not saying anything. I figure she hasn't heard it. It's the kind of thing you might mention. Although I notice I'm not mentioning it to her even though I *definitely* heard it.

Or did I?

I mean, come on, a *lion*?

Apart from the total freaking impossibility of the thing, and the absolute concrete fact that there are *no* lions, African or otherwise, in Scorpion Falls and never have been, there's already a whole famous book about a lion in the back of a wardrobe. It's a movie too. I've seen it.

So I know what I do next.

Feeling more stupid than scared, I reach out a hand towards the back of the wardrobe. I brace myself, expecting — correction, *knowing* — a secret door to another world will swing open when I make contact. My hand stretches out, millimetre by millimetre, until my fingers touch the smooth wood and —

Someone taps my shoulder and I scream like I've been electrocuted.

'What are you *doing*?' Ari hisses and jumps back, looking at me like I'm some kind of dipshit, which is understandable because I probably am.

I scramble out of the wardrobe, trying my best to seem like I hadn't been trying to open the gateway to a mystical kingdom ruled by lions, situated in the back of the wardrobe in Room 42 of the Iguana Motel.

'Um,' I say. 'Just, y'know . . . looking. For stuff.'

'You were sort of *stroking* the back of the wardrobe,' says Ari. 'And you were all tense, like you'd found something.' She peers at me closely and her voice softens. 'You *did* find something, didn't you, Theo? You look like you've seen a ghost. What was it? What did you see? Did you see a ghost?'

I can't tell her. I just *can't*. It's already bad enough she knows I saw Coley Briggs vanish and reappear; that I saw a girl who no one else seems to have heard of get swiped into a mystery maintenance cupboard and then vanish; that my mum (who might be lying about having multiple sclerosis) put *eyeballs* in a guest's room. If I add anything about finding Narnia at the back of Frank Maker's wardrobe, Ari's going to flip for real.

'What was it?' she asks again, this time more insistently. 'It doesn't matter how dumb you think it is, tell me!'

I turn away, trying to buy time.

And then I spot something.

At the back of a shelf in the wardrobe, a glint of light on metal. My stumbling exit from the wardrobe must've moved things around.

'That,' I say, nodding towards the metallic gleam.

'What is it?' says Ari, leaning closer.

I step forward and peer into the darkness. 'Not sure,' I say. 'There's a hidden compartment in here.'

'Grab it!' says Ari.

'You grab it! Could be, I dunno, a snake in there!'

Ari pauses. 'A snake?'

Given I was about to tell Ari I'd just heard a full-grown African lion behind the wardrobe, a snake inside the secret compartment sounds more than believable to me. But Ari's giving me that 'I'm disappointed in you' look so I reach inside the possibly snake-infested, possibly lion-infested secret compartment as bravely as I can and pull out a gold chain with a skull-shaped locket attached.

Ari picks up the necklace and lets it dangle in front of her, the light dancing across the gold. 'Pretty,' she murmurs. 'And creepy.'

'What's inside the locket?' I ask.

Holding the skull locket in the palm of her hand, Ari presses the clasp. The lid of the locket flicks open and inside is a photograph of an unsmiling dark-haired teenage girl.

Lani Lanchester.

Nineteen

'Lani!' I blurt out.

Ari looks down at the photo in the locket. 'That's her?' she says and I nod.

Ari frowns. 'She's pretty.'

'I guess. I didn't notice.'

'Very pretty.'

I look at Ari closely. 'Are you . . . jealous?' I say. 'You didn't think this girl *existed* until two seconds ago!'

'She's still pretty,' hisses Ari. 'And anyway, I'm not jealous!'

'Stop!' I say.

'I will not stop,' says Ari. 'I —'

'No!' I say, louder. 'Stop, I heard something outside!'

Scampering to the blinds, I peek through. *Don't be him, don't be him, don't be him.* My stomach lurches like I'm on a tinny in a Category 4 cyclone.

'It's him, isn't it?' says Ari.

'Of course it's him!' I hiss. 'I knew this would happen!'

Frank Maker, carrying a heavy-looking black sports bag, steps out of a white van at the motel entrance.

'We gotta go!' I say but it's too late. Maker's already heading back to 42. We're well and truly trapped.

Stuffing the locket in my pocket, I look around the room for somewhere to hide. There's really only one choice.

The wardrobe.

Ari pulls me inside and closes the door, neither of us saying a word. Scooting behind the hanging clothes, we try our very best to breathe through our ears. I can feel the blood pounding through my veins and wonder if I'm about to have a heart attack. Ari holds my hand tightly and I suddenly feel a lot better. Not *confident* about the outcome exactly (which is still looking massively, massively *bad*), just a little happier that at least we're in this together. I squeeze Ari's hand, she squeezes back and, just for a second or two, I'm almost *glad* we ended up hiding inside creepy Frank's wardrobe.

Almost.

All my mushy feel-good vibes evaporate instantly the second the door to Room 42 opens and Frank puts down his sports bag. He grunts as he does this, like the bag is too heavy, and a nasty thought pops into my head: *That's Lani in the bag!* Oh, Sweet Baby Cheeses! Please don't let that be so, please, please, please.

I strain to hear more sounds but there's just dead, super-scary silence.

What's he doing?

I sense Ari is thinking exactly the same as me. It's dark inside the wardrobe — *no kidding?* — but there's enough light coming through the cracks at the side of the doors for us to see a little. Neither of us dare look at each other in case we make a sound. I start fixating on the idea that I'm going to sneeze. Like, I'm definitely *not* going to sneeze, but as soon as I let the word 'sneeze' into my brain it's all I can think about.

A shadow passes in front of the wardrobe as Frank moves into the bathroom. A tap starts running and Frank washes his hands. When he's done, the shower goes on and Ari squeezes my hand. I know what she's thinking: if Maker gets into the shower, we can slip out.

I squeeze back. *Good thinking.*

Frank comes back into the room. We can't see much of him except flashes of movement as he passes in front of the wardrobe, but we can tell he's getting undressed. Makes sense since he's about to shower but the thought makes me sick. The only thing worse than being discovered hiding in the wardrobe by Frank Maker would be being discovered hiding in the wardrobe by a naked Frank Maker. I figure Ari's got the same idea because her grip on my hand tightens.

But the wardrobe doors stay closed.

'It's me,' says Frank and I practically faint before I realise he's speaking into his phone. My movement causes a couple of hangers on the rail to move a tiny fraction but there's no noise.

I think.

Ari and I stand like statues while we wait for Frank to speak again.

'Yes,' says Frank into the phone, 'all checked. All taken care of. That avenue is sealed. We move on.'

There's a pause. Then Frank speaks again.

'The kid? You think? K said he'd shut that down.'

K? Could that be Principal Kenwright? And, if that's the case, am I 'the kid'? Why would I be 'the kid'? And what, exactly, is 'shutting that down'?

'Tonight,' says Frank. 'In darkness. Yeah. Out.'

We hear the phone being put down on the bedside table and I hope Ari hadn't left any signs she'd been searching. Frank pads across to the bathroom and closes the door. The sound of the shower running decreases and a soft click tells us he's opened and closed the cubicle door. We wait a few moments until we're totally sure Frank's in the shower.

'Now,' I whisper to Ari.

Ari lets go of my hand and, as gently and quietly as she can, eases open the wardrobe door. The noise of the shower increases and Ari peers out cautiously. She steps towards the door and suddenly the shower goes off. Ari races to the door of Room 42 while I, caught in two minds, step back inside the wardrobe just as the door to the bathroom opens. I've only got time to glimpse Ari outside before I close the wardrobe door again. It's a close thing.

Frank comes out of the bathroom and moves across to the window. I can't see what he's doing, but I sense he's suspicious. I can hear him opening the slats of the blinds and I hope Ari's made it out of sight.

Everything goes real quiet for a second or two and then I can hear Maker get close to the wardrobe door. Too close. I slide as far back as I can as the door starts to open. There's nowhere left for me to go.

This is it. He's got me.

An image of the heavy black sports bag flashes through my head. And then, just as I'm wondering if it's going to hurt when I become the next Lani Lanchester, the wood panel behind me silently slides open and I fall backwards into pitch darkness so total and absolute I might as well be in a coffin.

Twenty

The dark doesn't stop being any less dark when I open my eyes. In fact, it's still so completely and totally black, I reach up and check with my fingertips that my eyelids are actually open. That saying about not being able to see your hand in front of your face? Well, that's me right now.

After I fell out of the back of Frank Maker's wardrobe, I must have hit the deck pretty hard and knocked myself out. Least, that's what I assume when I come around, but I have to consider the possibility that I'm, y'know, *dead* and that this darkness thing is what being dead is like. Just absolutely dark, all the time. I don't know what I imagined the afterlife would be like but if I had to take a stab, I'd have figured there'd be a *bit* more happening in the way of clouds and angels, or maybe if I was less lucky, fire and pain and all that. If I *am* dead, then the most I can say about the afterlife is it smells of grease and is a little on the chilly side. And here's another thing: the afterlife also has a floor cos I'm a hundred percent lying on *something*.

I put my hand down and touch bare concrete.

That's a good development because if I can feel something solid — and I can totally tell it's concrete — then maybe I'm not dead. Or completely out of my mind.

I'm just starting to feel a little better when the lion roars.

This time the thing's so close I can practically feel its breath. Pure panic grips me from head to toe. If I thought the idea of being discovered hiding in Frank's wardrobe was scary, now I know what being truly scared is. Truly being scared means being trapped in a dark concrete box with an angry lion. Another possibility pings. This isn't the afterlife; this is Narnia. Except, I remind myself, Narnia doesn't exist, seeing it's a book written by someone I'd need to look up on my —

Phone!

The word explodes in my brain.

Phone! I have a phone! And my phone has a —

I scramble the phone torch on and hold the beam out like it's a fricken' light sabre or a flame-thrower or something that'll put the lion off eating me.

Massive relief number one is I can't see any lions.

Massive relief number two is I'm probably not dead because there's a red metal sign bolted to a wall next to me containing the words *DUCT 16/03245. Int/Alt reference G2*. No idea what that means but it doesn't sound much like Narnia, or the afterlife. Then, in smaller print at the bottom, it says *Contractor: Mackay Hydraulics for Medullo Industries*. So, unless there's a Mackay Hydraulics and a Medullo Industries in the afterlife, I'm not dead.

The next big question is about where I am. And, if this isn't Narnia, why there's a lion knocking around. Knowing the lion isn't in the tiny concrete box with me is A Very Good Thing — obviously — but the fact remains there's still a lion much closer to me than I'm comfortable with. I don't know about you, but I prefer my African lions to be at least two continents away from me at all times.

I get to my feet and try to make sense of my surroundings.

The box is about three metres square and made of concrete. Every surface is covered in a thick layer of grease-clogged dust. Above me the box disappears upwards into inky blackness which not even the torch beam can penetrate. In one corner of the concrete box, a square piece of iron is set into the floor and hinged on one side with a latched handle on the other. I take a step forward to open it but then suddenly stop, realising there's a definite possibility the lion might be underneath. A sudden vision of me dropping directly into the lion's open jaws flicks into my head. It's not a good thought, so I forget about the hatch for the time being and see if there's anything else I've missed. Maybe there's a way back into Room 42. Another portal. Maybe Frank Maker's gone out again and I can get back to the Iggy, which now feels like the most desirable spot on the entire planet.

Sweeping the beam of the phone torch up and around every millimetre of the walls, I can't see anything that looks like it could be the back of a wardrobe. At this point I realise I'm holding a phone in my hand and not just a torch. I can just *call* Ari or, I dunno, call the cops, or the Army, or Mission Impossible; *someone* to come get me.

I pull up Ari's number but can't get a connection. I try again but get the same result. The phone battery is almost gone. The torch won't last much longer. The idea of being stuck down here in the pitch dark makes me feel sick.

Squatting on the dirty concrete, I do my best to come up with a plan. Trouble is, coming up with a plan usually means having something to work with and I haven't got much except —

The hatchway.

It might have an angry lion underneath it, but it looks very much like it's a choice between the hatch or staying in the concrete box until I die. And, since I much prefer breathing to not breathing, I don't have an option.

At the hatchway I put my ear to the metal. No getting away from it, the lion's definitely still under there, but unless I want to stay in this dirty concrete box forever, I have to try.

The heavy iron hatch swings upwards with a metallic groan and a rush of warmer air pours through the black opening which resembles — far too closely for my liking — a great big gaping mouth. The kind of gaping mouth you might find on, for example, a massive freaking lion.

Pointing the torch into the darkness, I risk a peek inside, expecting at any moment to become lion lunch.

There's no lion — thank you, Baby Cheeses! — but the torch beam picks out a tonne of other stuff: a spaghetti of pipes and cables bolted to one wall, and a massive winch mounted on a solid steel floor above a black hole. The lion roars again as the winch turns and I finally get it. There's no lion, no Narnia, just a plain old winch.

A thick cable coils neatly round the winch's central column. The rush of air from below increases and something hurtles towards me from the blackness below like a killer whale powering up from the ocean depths. I suddenly realise exactly where I am.

I'm at the top of an industrial lift shaft.

With the lift hurtling towards me at full speed.

Twenty-One

I've seen this movie before.

Some guy's trapped in a lift shaft and the thing stops at the last moment just as he thinks he's gonna get smashed? Well, that's the situation I'm in now, except I've already figured out the lift isn't going to smash into the winch.

It's not that I'm cocky or anything but, I mean, what would be the point of that? Whoever built the lift didn't design it so it gets smashed every time it gets used, right? So when the lift comes towards me I don't panic too much. Don't get me wrong. I'm not saying I'm totally cool about it, but I'm a hundred percent sure (okay, maybe ninety-eight point three percent sure) that this thing will stop before it hit the winch.

Which it does. Go me. Yay.

Now comes the really brave part. I've got to clamber down past the winch, with just enough space between me and the cable drum to squeeze through. I'm praying the lift doesn't start up again too soon because, if it does, it's gonna drag me straight into the winch guts and I really don't fancy my chances if that happens.

I make it past the cable drum and ease through a gap at the side of the steel plate holding the winch above the top of the lift. It's a short drop to the roof of the lift and that's where the second nasty thought pops up. If the lift starts now with me on top it'll —

The lift lurches and drops like a stone. I lose my balance and, for one horrible, horrible second, I almost roll off one side and get creamed by the concrete wall of the shaft moving past me in a sickening blur. Scrabbling desperately, my fingers latch onto a metal bar on top of the lift and I pull myself back just in time. Flattening myself against the steel roof, we plummet down through the darkness, the lift shaft lights flickering past.

How far down does this thing go?

With a grinding noise like a tonne of rocks being dropped into a woodchipper, the lift brakes slam on, instantly relocating my stomach to somewhere north of my scalp. Drenched in sweat, my fingers clamp so tightly to the iron bar I can't feel them anymore. Only the thought that the lift might take me back up at any moment — I have a sudden image of me being yo-yoed up and down the lift shaft for the rest of my life — forces me to prise my fingers loose and search for a way to get into the lift compartment itself.

There's another hatch to my left but it's bolted

shut. I pull on the thing with every bit of strength I've got (admittedly not very much) but it doesn't matter anyway because the hatch is sealed tighter than a schoolteacher's wallet.

A beam of light to my right indicates a gap of about thirty centimetres between the lift and the concrete shaft. I could, I reckon, just about wriggle through and swing myself down from there into the lift. The problem is, just like with the cable winch earlier, if this thing moves while I'm halfway through, I'll be smushed against the concrete like a bug on a windshield. Nice choice, huh?

There's nothing for it but to try. Right now. 'Get moving, Sumner,' I mutter under my breath.

I drop my legs down first and then push my hips through the gap. Now I'm hanging half in and half out of the lift. I drop down until my chin is at the same level as the lift roof. Above me I hear a distant clanking sound and the lift sort of shudders.

It's getting ready to move. Smushed? Stuck this way I could get cut in two.

With panic rising to epic levels, I ease my head into the gap between the lift roof and the shaft wall.

And get completely stuck.

Twenty-two

I learn two things fast about Theo Sumner in the next two seconds.

First is that I *seriously* do not want to get my head crushed by an industrial lift. I'm guessing most of the world's population feels the same way about getting their head crushed by an industrial lift so that's no big surprise.

The second thing I discover is that my head is made of solid rubber. It must be because as soon as the head-crushing starts becoming a definite possibility, I find I can pull my head through the gap quite easily so long as I don't mind scraping my face against the concrete. As the choice is between getting my entire head crushed and having a bit of skin scraped off, I take the skin scraping option.

With my head free, I drop into the empty lift just as it falls once again.

Blood running down one side of my face, I slump, panting, against the wall of the lift and try to recover. My ears pop. My stomach lurches. By my calculations, we must be close to the Earth's core by now.

Eventually, the lift jerks to a stop and somehow, don't ask me how, I know we've reached rock bottom. I also figure the lift is probably on some sort of automatic timer which means all I have to do is wait and I'll get a ride right back up to where I came from. And then I think: which is where, exactly, genius? The back of the wardrobe in Room 42? Narnia? Where the hell am I?

Maybe that's it.

Maybe I am in actual Hell. The full hit; Satan, demons, fiery pits and eternal punishment. But then I remember the plate bolted to the lift shaft: *Contractor: Mackay Hydraulics for Medullo Industries.* I'm not in Narnia, or Hell. I'm in a Medullo Industries Mine six hours west of Mackay in Queensland.

It's obvious really, now I think about it. Scorpion Falls is, after all, a mining town. The whole place is basically sitting on top of a network of tunnels and mine shafts and whatnot. Most of the mining is strip mining: mining done at the surface by digging down and hauling the coal straight out of the earth. But there's still plenty of mining in Scorpi done the old way by digging tunnels and shafts.

So, all I have to do is tell someone I'm down here and I'll get taken up to the surface, right?

Yeah, dumbass, and then they'll give you cookies and ice-cream and everything will be aces and you'll get tucked up in bed at night and no one's gonna ask any awkward questions about Uncle Frank and the wardrobe and Coley Briggs and Lani being missing and the *spooky black kitbag in Room 42*.

Get a grip, Sumner! Kids are disappearing! Photos are getting retouched, stuff is being covered up and weird guys with spooky eyes are driving around in white vans. Add in the fact that there's a secret Narnia-type gateway to Hell in the back of Frank's wardrobe, *plus* you already suspect Frank of doing away with Lani Lanchester, *and* he's involved in whatever-the-hell-that-all-was with Coley Briggs, the lift doesn't represent safety, not by a long chalk.

This is not normal. If things were normal, how was it exactly I managed to get from the back of a wardrobe into a Medullo Industries lift shaft? It sure isn't Narnia down here. This whole thing is as real as a toothache, as freaky as Halloween and about as wholesome as roadkill. Trusting Frank Maker to do the right thing would be like a toddler in the woods asking a starving grizzly to take him back to Mummy. No, whatever happens I've got to at least try and sneak myself out of here.

The doors to the lift rattle open.

Directly in front of me is a rack of steel lockers and some scuzzy old dials bolted to a rock wall. A huge sloping tunnel curves away downwards to the right and rises up on the left. Pipes line the tunnel walls like veins. The air is damp and it's as cold as a coffin down here. I can almost feel the weight of billions of tonnes of rock pushing down above me. Water drips atmospherically from the tunnel roof, tapping out a metallic rhythm on the steel lockers. *Bonk. Boink. Boink.* The whole place vibrates with the sound of clanking machinery and air vents hissing like cats. The black tunnel walls gleam wetly. Alien-looking green streaks stain the rock. It's about as welcoming an environment as the surface of freaking Mars and is *totally* the kind of place where some goop-dripping alien monster with a trillion teeth would be slithering around. I mean, that kind of thing is aces when you see it on TV but when you're actually *in* that kind of situation? It *sucks*.

A large yellow sign above the lockers reads M8ER WD10 LEVEL 19. CATEGORY 6 SITE. EXTREME DANGER: BREATHING APPARATUS COMPULSORY. HARD HATS COMPULSORY.

'Extreme Danger'? That can't be good. And there's something else funny about the sign. That bit at the start — 'M8ER WD10' — wasn't that the rego number on the white van that picked up Coley Briggs? How does creepy bloke's rego end up on the wall of a Medullo Industries mine? The truth is, I don't know. Could be a coincidence I suppose but I'm always seeing detectives on TV talking about not believing in coincidences. 'M8ER' is pretty close to 'Maker'. Or maybe not. If you say the 8 out loud it sounds like 'Mater'. What does that mean? Not for the first time I feel my brain throbbing painfully and file the 'coincidence' away.

While I'm hesitating at the lift entrance the ground begins to tremble, and an enormous tip truck appears, labouring silently up the slope. This truck isn't like any truck I've seen in Scorpi before either. It's just a great big metal box resting on six tyres, each twice my height. The thing looks like it's being controlled remotely, or maybe on some sort of automatic system. How would I know? I can't see a driver is what I'm trying to say.

The driverless truck, filled to the brim with rocks, hums past in a cloud of dust, its yellow warning light strobing the tunnel as it disappears from view.

With my hand across my mouth, I step into the dust-filled tunnel and take a few cautious steps away from the lift. I'm going left; the same direction as the truck, figuring that way I'll have more chance of finding someone who doesn't look like they're gonna put me in a black kitbag. In my mind, the lift represents Frank Maker, so that's not really an option. I'll take my chances down here.

By now I'm fifty metres down the tunnel at the point where the curve is starting to take the lift out of view. I take a quick look back. Frank Maker or not, that lift is still the only thing that connects me to the surface and I'm kind of reluctant to let it out of my sight. I go a few more paces and the noise level picks up a notch. Up ahead the tunnel splits into two directions. There are no handy maps nearby, or anything like that to give me a clue about which one I should take.

I peer down the left tunnel but don't see anything I can use to make a decision. Same with the right-hand tunnel.

While I'm standing there feeling like a complete tool, I hear an electric crackle and, for the first time, notice a dust-coated TV screen bolted to the rock. I wipe some of the dirt off to reveal a CCTV monitor flicking through a number of cameras. Just for a moment the screen comes to life and I flash on an image of a gleaming steel blade coming right at me out of a blinding white background.

'Aaargh!' I yell and jump backwards. The image is so clear I check myself for cuts but there's nothing; it's just a picture on the lousy screen. When I check the CCTV screen it's gone back to showing the underground tunnels. I'm beginning to think I imagined the whole thing when something else appears onscreen, coming towards me fast.

This time it's not a steel blade. It's a spider running along one of the tunnels.

A spider the size of a freaking labrador.

Twenty-three

There's no way of knowing which tunnel the giant spider's in — there are codes on the screens but that's not much use unless you know what those codes mean. The giant spider clomping towards me could be coming from either tunnel and will be *right here* any second now. I'm too far away from the lift to make it back there before the spider arrives and does whatever freaking monster spiders do. I'm betting it's not good.

So it's simple, I have to choose a tunnel.

Or fight. It might be a ridiculous idea but I consider it anyway. I look around for something to use as a weapon but can't see anything even close. In desperation, I search my pockets and my fingers touch the secret stone Ari gave me back at the Iggy. I'd forgotten all about it what with all the wardrobe/Narnia/Frank and the kitbag horrors. It's too small to use, but I pull it out anyway and look at it for the first time.

It's a smooth, light grey river pebble. It might annoy a small mouse if I threw it really hard. It wasn't going to stop a psycho giant spider for a microsecond.

But.

Written on the pebble in black marker pen is one word: 'RIGHT!'

I waste absolutely zero time thinking about *how* Ari would know I'd need help or how she knew I'd look at the pebble at that exact moment. Instead, I sprint flat out down the right-hand tunnel, running like my life depends on it. Because it does.

If I've chosen the wrong tunnel, if Ari's secret stone is just some nonsense, I'll run straight into the giant freaking spider but now the dice have been thrown, and I'm committed totally to following Ari's secret pebble instructions. Ari's secret stone buys me some time but not much. The right-hand tunnel *is* spider free but I hear the faint *clitter-clatter* of the eight-legged monster changing direction. It knows where I am and, as fast as I'm running, there's no way I'm gonna outrun a giant freaking spider. Eight legs against two, see?

Racing round the curve I see an open lift straight ahead. A little prayer becomes a kind of chant as I run, my footsteps beating out the rhythm on the rock floor.

Don't let the doors shut and I'll be good forever.
Don't let the doors shut and I'll be good forever.
Don't let the doors shut and I'll be good forever.

When I'm still twenty metres away the doors start

to shut. *But I said I'd be good forever!*

The spider's coming up behind me real quick now. I pull on a reserve of speed I didn't know I had and scream as I hurl myself headfirst at the rapidly closing gap. My shoulder clangs hard against the door but I get through. Just. Landing hard, I skid painfully across the lift floor and slam straight into the back wall. I'm dazed, but not too dazed I don't register the lift doors clanging shut behind me. Somewhere above my head a lion roars again and the lift creaks into life. *Come on, come on, come on!*

Outside, judging by the thunder of approaching footsteps, the spider is closing fast.

BAM! Something MASSIVE buckles the solid metal, shaking me and the lift. I reach up and slam the palm of my hand on the 'UP' button.

It doesn't respond.

And now a pointed black spider leg appears in the crack between the lift doors, quickly followed by a second, then a third. As the doors start to peel apart, I back myself against the far wall of the lift, my legs weak with fear, and realise that I'm spider food.

The doors open fully and the spider looks at me.

It scuttles into the lift and the doors close. Me and the spider start moving upwards.

Twenty-four

You ever been trapped deep underground in a small lift with a giant spider? If not, I definitely do not recommend the experience.

What had I been *thinking* about wandering around down there in the bowels of Hell? Exactly who did I think I was? Some sort of Scorpi Falls Sherlock planning to solve the whole thing myself? A muscle-bound action movie hero? Superman? Yup, all of the above dumb ideas, which means I'm about to be wolfed down like a late-night pizza from Vinny's.

The spider takes a step forward and I calm down enough to start noticing some things about it.

The first thing is that it's not, strictly speaking, an actual spider.

When I say that, what I mean is that it's not *organic*. This thing is made of metal, is painted bright red, and has the words *Medullo Research/ARACH16* printed along one side of its body, together with a cluster of technical looking lenses and lights and whatnot whirring away on top of its head.

In other words, the spider is a robot.

Robo-spider steps closer. Then, very carefully, almost like it's enjoying itself, the spider lifts one of its sharp metallic legs and begins moving the point precisely towards my head. I freeze, staring at the finely polished spike as it gets closer and closer to me.

This is it. I know it. The End of Theo Sumner. Skewered by an underground psycho robo-spider. Never saw that one coming. I mean, you wouldn't, would you?

The spider's leg reaches a spot directly in front of my eyes and I haven't moved a centimetre. I wonder if it's going to hurt. My guess is a solid 'yes' on that one.

Just as I'm contemplating a last second Kung Fu move, the top of the spider's leg sort of peels open. A small camera lens extends from inside and scans my face with a blue-white light.

Satisfied, the spider sort of settles down while — I assume — it checks whatever data it's picked up about me. I still haven't moved. To test if the spider is triggered by motion, I take a step to one side and immediately the spider rears up, lights flickering and hydraulics whirring. How I don't poop my pants right there and then I can't explain, but it was a close call.

The thing scans me once more and this time I really try not to move. I may not move ever again if it means keeping this thing off me.

ARACH16 settles back, watching me.

The lift keeps rising.

As we zoom upwards, I solemnly promise myself that if I ever get out of here, I'm going to forget all about what's been happening in Scorpion Falls. All of it. Everything. Let the cops sort it out. No more robo-spiders. No more investigations. No more me doing anything exciting in any way. *If* I get out. *If* I make it back to the surface. Up top there must be at least one responsible adult who won't have homicidal thoughts in my direction. Stands to reason. Whatever's up there has got to be a better bet than the robo-spider down here in Hell.

Eventually, just as I start to think I can't stay motionless a second longer, the spider inserts the point of another leg into a socket on the lift control panel. About three seconds later, the lift stops and the doors slide open to reveal total darkness. No light of any kind. No gleam of daylight in the distance. Just a solid black wall of dark so intense I feel I could reach out and touch it. It's so complete that even the light from the lift doors doesn't extend three centimetres into the blackness. I've never seen a black hole in space but I'm pretty sure this would be what one looked like.

I look at the spider, unsure — again — of what to do for the best. *No change there, then*, says my annoying inner voice.

Sometimes I hate that inner voice. Now is one of those times.

A booming wail from some unidentified machine

below my feet reminds me it won't be long before this lift heads straight back down again. The robot-spider just stands there, a few lights blinking on what I've come to think of as its face.

That makes up my mind. I take a small step forward and the robo-spider scuttles to one side. *Go on*, it seems to be saying, *out you go*. I edge past the thing, expecting at any moment for one of its pointed arms to shoot out and pin me to the lift wall. But it doesn't move.

I get past the spider, take a blind step forward out of the lift into darkness, and fall straight back into Room 42.

Twenty-five

The only change I can see when I hit the carpet in Room 42 is that there's no sign of Frank Maker. That, and the fact that the room is filled with cops. Three to be exact.

To say the cops are surprised to see a dirty, bleeding, teenage boy fall out of the motel wardrobe would be quite an understatement. I'd been in the legendary Scorpi High history class when Coley Briggs snuck a python into Mrs Sweeney's briefcase. I never thought *anything* could top Mrs Sweeney's reaction to reaching inside her case and finding a metre-long snake with a serious attitude problem until I witnessed the effect of my sudden appearance in Room 42 at the Iggy. All three of the cops in 42 jump about five metres in the air, scream like little babies and (unlike babies) start swearing before they all pull out massive freaking guns and scream at me to *get on the ground right now!*

'Uh,' I squeak, 'I am on the ground?'

'GET ON THE GROUND RIGHT NOW!' yells one of the cops as if I hadn't spoken, so I try and get even more on the ground than I already am. Basically that involves me shutting my eyes tightly and pressing my face as far as it can possibly go into the incredibly scratchy motel carpet. There's not much more I can do.

'He's already on the ground, Brenno,' says another cop. This guy sounds older and much less freaked out which is exactly what you want when you have panicky cops pointing big guns at you. In that kind of situation it is always way better for NO ONE to be freaking out in any way whatsoever.

'YEAH, WELL!' says Brenno, apparently still not entirely convinced that I'm enough on the ground for his liking. He gives me a kind of prod with the toe of his boot to keep me down, like I'm about to spring some secret martial arts moves on him.

'YOU *ARMED?*' screams the third cop who, so far, hasn't said anything. 'YOU CARRYING ANY WEAPONS? I SAID, ARE YOU CARRYING ANY WEAPONS?'

'No! No, no, no!' I scream back. 'No weapons! No weapons! Don't shoot! Don't shoot!'

'Put your hands behind your back, kid,' says the older-voiced cop. I do as he says and I feel someone put handcuffs on me. As soon as that's done, I feel the tension in the room deflate. You can almost hear the *pffft*.

Someone pulls me into a sitting position, my hands still cuffed behind my back and the three cops stare at me like I'm a Martian.

The first cop, the one nearest me, is tall with blond hair, and looks like he's gonna hurl. His name tag reads 'Fleming'. The second is a chunkier older cop called Driver (name tag again) and the third — Brennigan, the shouty one — has black hair and gives the strong impression he still wants to straight out shoot me. I've never seen any of them before in Scorpi.

'You ever see anything like that?' says Brennigan. He holsters his gun, bends over and puts his hands on his knees, and kind of blows out a long sigh. 'Jeeezus! Kid just flew outta there! Whammo! I never seen anything like that! You ever see anything like that?'

'Check the wardrobe, Brenno,' says Driver.

Brennigan pulls his weapon again and yanks open the wardrobe door like it's the front door of a Mexican drug lord's hideout. After a quick inspection he stands back. 'CLEAR!' he yells and I see Driver wince.

'Easy, tiger,' says Driver.

'Where'd you come from?' says Fleming, narrowing his eyes.

I try not to say the words 'the wardrobe', but I don't really have any choice. 'The wardrobe,' I say. 'Sir,' I add, just to show him I'm being a good boy and he doesn't have to shoot me.

'Don't get smart!' says Fleming. 'We already checked the wardrobe!'

The older cop rolls his eyes. 'We *saw* him come outta the wardrobe, Fleming. I mean, the kid *did* come out of the wardrobe. There's no debate about that.'

Brennigan moves closer and peers at me like I'm the eighth wonder of the world.

'Hey!' he says. 'I think this is the missing Sumner boy!'

There's an immediate reaction from the other two cops. They go from 'nervy' and 'trigger-happy' to 'concerned/excited' in about half a second.

'Doesn't look like the photos,' says Fleming. He takes out an A4 printed sheet with a photo on it and squints at me. 'Looks older than the photo.'

'They always do,' says Driver. 'On account of him, y'know, being older than when the photo was taken. Plus he's all banged up. And covered in grease.'

Driver turns and looks at me, concern written all over his face. In some ways it's more alarming than when he was flat out glaring at me. '*Are* you the Sumner kid?' he says in a low voice, as if I'm a deer about to skitter off into the woods. 'Are you Theo Sumner?'

I nod nervously. The older cop carries on staring at me before looking back at the photo.

'Jesus H Christ,' he whispers, shaking his head slowly from side to side. Driver reaches up to a radio mike clipped to his shirt and presses a button. 'Officer Driver at the Iguana. We have a positive ID on the missing Sumner kid.' There's a pause and then a crackle from someone on the other end.

'No, no sign of her. Correct,' says Driver. He looks at me again. 'Yeah. Him, deffo. Theo Sumner. Kid's got abrasions and he's pretty filthy but, as far as we can see, otherwise okay.' Driver breaks off from the conversation and nods to Fleming. 'Take those cuffs off him. Now!'

The handcuffs are unlocked and I stand up, rubbing my wrists.

'We need an ambulance,' says Driver into his radio. 'And a full crime scene unit. Get in touch with Brisbane Command and let them know. We have to lock this place down.'

Driver clicks the off switch and turns to me. 'Are you really okay, kid?' he says. 'After all this time?'

I frown. What the holy frick is this guy talking about? All what time?

'I'm okay,' I say. 'Face stings like crazy but I was only down th — only in there about half an hour.'

Driver glances at Fleming and Brennigan. *You hearing this?* says his expression. All three of the cops turn back to me.

'What did you say, Theo?' says Driver.

Now it's my turn to look puzzled. 'I said I've only been in the wardrobe about thirty minutes. Did I say something wrong?'

Driver clears his throat, puts a hand on my shoulder, and looks me straight in the eye.

'Theo,' he says, gently, 'you've been missing for a solid year. A year today.'

Twenty-six

I laugh.

'That's funny,' I say. 'Good one.' The fact is I don't think it's much of a joke AT ALL but I'm trying to buy some time to think.

But Driver doesn't laugh with me. Instead he — and this really frightens me — pats my shoulder sadly. *Not the shoulder pat!* I think. People only get patted on the shoulder like that when they are getting Very Bad News. I don't want to get Very Bad News.

'You really don't remember?' Driver says, softly. He gestures for me to sit down on the bed. 'You'd better take a seat.'

'Maybe they were drugging him or something like that,' says Fleming. 'Coma? Or maybe they were keeping him in some dungeon type thing?'

'He was in the wardrobe,' says Driver and winks at me in a kind of *see what I have to put up with?* way.

'Wait,' I say. 'This isn't a joke?'

'It certainly isn't,' says Driver. 'But we're glad we found you, Theo. Maybe you can help with the others.'

'Others?'

'Was anyone else in that . . . uh, wardrobe with you, Theo?' says Driver. 'Anyone we should be worried about back there besides you?'

After a second's hesitation, I shake my head. Ari doesn't need to be dragged into this. She's already in enough trouble with Kesha and Mina without me blabbing we'd been prowling around inside Frank Maker's wardrobe. Besides, technically, Ari *wasn't* with me in the wardrobe when I came out.

'No, no one,' I say.

Although he's nodding nicely enough, something in Officer Driver's face tells me he thinks I might not be telling the entire truth. Cops get lied to so much they get an ability to sniff a liar out real quick. They might not know what the exact truth is, but they sure as sugar know when *something's* being covered up.

Driver's reaction makes me wonder if I'm doing the right thing by not spilling. Ari might get in trouble with her parents but the cops need to know the details, don't they? This thing is bigger than me, bigger than me worrying about Ari or anything like that. The trouble is, where do I start? Lani Lanchester? Coley Briggs popping in and out of reality like a human *Whack-A-Mole* game? Robot freaking *spiders*? Or maybe I could spark up a discussion about the wormhole in the back of the wardrobe in Room 42 at the Iggy?

And that's without getting into the news that

— somehow — I'd been down that wormhole *for a year.* The thought makes me sick. Literally. I only just make it to the bathroom before I spew. *A year!* I spew again and again and again until there's nothing left. A cold sweat breaks out over every centimetre of my skin.

Driver pushes the bathroom door open a little. 'You okay, Theo?'

I push myself upright and flush. 'Uh-huh,' I grunt. To be honest I'm a long way from okay. I splash water on my face and head back into the motel room to wait for the ambulance. Puking has made me entirely reconsider my silence and I decide to tell Driver everything I know.

'Uh, back in there I —' I begin but Driver doesn't hear and cuts me off mid-sentence.

'Don't say anything. Not yet. The best thing is to get you patched up at the hospital and we can get a proper statement at the station,' he says. 'The Task Force will be flying in from Brissy and they'll want to know everything. They don't want me stuffing things up by having you blurt anything out.'

'The Task Force?' I say.

'Us locals don't have the resources, Theo,' says Driver. 'Not when there's this many cases and it's been going on so long.'

'How many, uh, cases?'

'Eight kids gone,' chimes in Fleming. 'Biggest murde — uh, missing persons case in Queensland history.' He's almost smiling, like he really wants to blurt out *woah, check out little old Scorpi Falls!* 'Wait,' he carries on as something occurs to him, 'it's only seven, now you're back.' He does his best not to sound disappointed the murder score has come down.

'This'll be big news,' says Officer Driver. 'And, to be honest, you're the first good news we've had on this one for a while.'

A flashing blue light sweeps the room.

'Your lift,' says Driver. The other two cops are still gawping at me like an exhibit in a zoo. *See The Amazing Kid Who Came Back From The Dead!*

I glance over at the wardrobe and Brennigan, following my gaze, steps across and peers inside suspiciously, his hand on his pistol.

'Still reckon there's something funny 'bout this wardrobe,' he says.

No kidding.

The door to the room opens and two paramedics walk in followed by Principal Kenwright and a middle-aged woman I don't recognise.

'Hello, Theo,' says Kenwright, softly. 'Good to see you again. It really is.'

I don't really know what to say so I don't say anything. *Kenwright?* What's he doing here?

'Hi, Theo,' says one of the paramedics. 'Can we take a quick look at you before we get going? Just make sure there are no injuries that need immediate treatment. Is that okay?' She's also speaking super softly when she talks to me and I realise everyone is doing the same. It's starting to freak me out.

While the paramedics deal with the scrape on my face and check I've got all my legs and arms or whatever, I watch Kenwright and the middle-aged woman huddle with Driver. They're obviously talking about me because they keep flicking glances in my direction and smiling. A lot. It's those weak smiles that worry me.

'We're good to go,' says the paramedic. 'Don't think there's much wrong but let's get you checked out properly, hey?' She helps me to my feet and the two of them walk me to the door. The cops and Kenwright and the middle-aged woman all stand back to let us through, Driver patting me on the shoulder as I pass. 'Take care, Theo,' he says. 'We'll come by later for a proper statement, okay?'

'Yeah, sure,' I say.

I'm feeling really crook now and the paramedics sense it too. They hurry me to the open doors of the ambulance. I know if I don't lie down soon I'm gonna fall down. One of the paramedics start talking into his radio, letting the hospital know we're on the way. 'East Gate,' I hear the medic say. 'Fifteen minutes.'

The cops and Kenwright are sort of standing around waiting for the ambulance to go. To my right a cluster of motel guests are rubbernecking and, behind them, Kesha and Mina standing stone-faced at the entrance to Reception. There's no sign of

Ari and the Patels don't exactly seem overjoyed I've reappeared.

As I'm being strapped onto the gurney in the ambulance I glance back at Room 42. I'm fading fast but, through the open doors of the motel room, I see the middle-aged woman check that no one's watching, then open the wardrobe door and step inside. She closes the door behind her.

She doesn't come out.

Twenty-seven

Radio chatter. The static crackles, competing with the noise of the ambulance engine. I lift my head from the gurney and the paramedic gently pushes me back down.

'Easy, Theo,' she says, still using that sing-song voice people only use when they're talking to toddlers or invalids. She has a syringe in her hand and she sticks it in my arm. 'Just a sedative,' she says. 'To keep you calm.'

I think: *I'm already calm.*

But, like, whatever. The stuff in the paramedic's syringe flows through my veins like warm honey. Nice. My eyelids become impossibly heavy. I turn to look through the sliver of window I can see. We go past the Maccas at the Woody Road junction and I briefly wonder why the ambulance is taking the back way to Bullreedy.

And then I sink back into a wonderful fog.

When I open my eyes it's just like one of those movie scenes when some bloke wakes up in hospital. Which is not exactly surprising as that's what's happening. For a while — a few minutes? A week? After the news of my missing year, the idea of time passing has become a little more fluid in my universe — I just lie there staring at the white ceiling and wait for the real me to come back.

Eventually I raise my head and take a look around.

There's a large bright strip light directly above my bed and a pale green curtain shutting me off from the rest of the ward. All the usual hospital type material is there: bits of equipment I don't recognise, a smell of disinfectant, people talking softly, the clank of trolleys, the beep beep of medical monitors.

A nurse appears around the curtain. She registers I'm awake and then disappears without a word.

I wait some more. I've never been in hospital before but I'm starting to realise there might be a significant amount of hanging around involved. I'm not planning on being in here very long. I only have a few scrapes and bruises.

And that's when the first alarm bell sounds in my head.

I only have a few scrapes and bruises.

If that's the case — and it is — why did I need to be sedated? And why am I lying in a hospital bed? Okay, I felt sick back in Room 42 but that was probably like shock or something, right? I'd just been told I'd skipped a year so, y'know, wasn't that a normal reaction? Did I really need to be hospitalised?

Still no sign of the nurse coming back.

I sit up, pull back the sheets and swing my legs out of bed. They feel okay. *I* feel okay. As I go to stand up it hits me that I'm wearing pyjamas. Like the curtains, they're a sort of pale-green colour. If I'm wearing PJs that means someone undressed me; probably that nurse who just looked in.

I try and get my thoughts in some kind of order, which is tricky on account of the sedatives. I flash back to that glimpse of the Woody Road Maccas and wonder again why the ambulance wasn't on the main road to Bullreedy Hospital. It didn't make any kind of sense for the ambulance to be taking that route. In the big scheme of things it doesn't seem like a huge deal . . . but it's still a niggle. A lot of 'whys'. Why *that* route? Why the sedatives?

And who *was* that woman with Kenwright who got into the wardrobe? What possible motive would she have for doing something like that?

While I'm on the subject of Kenwright, what the hell was he *doing* showing up at the Iggy? Kenwright's a high school principal, not a rapid response cop. Did they call him as soon as they called the ambulance? It didn't make sense.

Of course, I could've been so woozy coming out of the wardrobe that all of that stuff isn't real. It's something I've got to consider. Then I remember

Kenwright's voice in the motel room and I know I'm not imagining that. He was *there*, bro, absolutely, no question. I put a hand up to my face and feel the bandage over the scrape on my face from when I'd been trapped in the lift shaft. It feels tender, sore. That pain is real too. That happened. This is happening.

I move across to the pale green curtains and take a peek.

I'm on a ward containing three other beds, all of them empty. At one end of the ward is an open door where I can see nurses moving around a desk doing all nurse-type things. Everything looks normal and I feel my paranoia tick down a notch or two.

Relax, I tell myself. You're over-thinking.

Nah. I'm not. Eyeballs, Frank, Lani, Coley Briggs, the wardrobe in 42, the robot-spider, Kenwright's pal getting into the wardrobe, *the missing year*. I'm not over-thinking what's been happening at all. If anything, I'm *under*-thinking.

Details. That's what I need right now. I need details. I'm a details kind of person. That's what people always say: Theo's an odd one. Geeky. Likes to know all the details. If I get some details, I can pick out any red flags. I need to speak to Mum, need to speak to Ari, find out what's been happening while I was 'gone'. Find out from Driver what the — Hey, wait a sec. Officer Driver. And Fleming and Brennigan. Red flags right there.

I'd never seen any of those cops before in my life.

I'm not saying I know everyone in Scorpi but, outside of the FIFOs and the Medullo Industries bigwigs, the list of people I haven't at least *seen* before in town is real small. Scorpi hasn't got a massive police force. Tony Clark I know by name and I could probably pick out practically every other Scorpi cop from photos.

But not Driver, Fleming or Brennigan.

I guess it's possible they're from outside Scorpi. Maybe this missing kids case has gotten everyone stirred up and reinforcements have come in? It makes sense. I downgrade the cop paranoia and move onto the next detail: the hospital. I can make sure exactly where I am. It'll be something. A detail.

At the opposite end of the ward from the door is a window. The blinds are drawn.

I tip-toe to the window and, after checking none of the nurses are looking, pull down one of the slats and peer through.

I've never been to Bullreedy — like I said before, I wasn't even born there — but as soon as I look through the window I can tell you one thing: I haven't left Scorpion Falls.

Twenty-eight

Where I am is about four floors up, looking out across a large carpark dotted with vehicles. A tree-lined driveway leading off to the right ends at an entry gate coming off the main road. The entry gate has a guard house to one side and a red-and-white-striped boom across the road.

To my left is a row of bland-looking white office buildings, each of them four storeys high. A larger building, clearly the main one, stands two storeys higher and a spiky cluster of radio aerials and satellite dishes juts up from its roof like a Mohican haircut.

The whole place is landscaped as perfectly as a posh golf course: lush green lawns, carefully-pruned trees lining neat gravel paths. Across to one side is a yellow helicopter landing pad and, further out, a long concrete runway. Two small jets parked near a steel hangar gleam in the afternoon sun.

On a path directly below me, two men wearing blue uniforms glide along in an electric buggy. They stop at a white pole with a CCTV camera at the top and start lifting out some tools. That's when I notice all the other CCTV cameras dotted around the grounds of the hospital. There are lots of them.

I've no way of knowing if what I'm looking at is normal. Maybe hospitals do have heaps of CCTV cameras. Here's what I *can't* see though: I can't see any ambulances, or signs pointing the way to different departments, or other patients coming in for treatment. There's not much that tells me this is a genuine hospital.

A semi-trailer rumbles along the main road past the entry gate, just like a million other semi-trailers I've seen around Scorpi with the Medullo Industries logo standing out in blue and white. The trailer passes the gate and, about two hundred metres along the road, makes a right onto a dusty service road. There's something real familiar about the buildings in the distance and then I realise why. I'm looking back at Scorpion Falls from a place I've never been inside.

I'm not in Bullreedy Hospital. I'm at the Medullo Industries Research Institute.

Twenty-nine

'Oh, you're up,' says a voice behind me that contains about as much warmth as a penguin's butt. 'That's probably not a good idea.'

It's the nurse who looked in through the curtain earlier. A second nurse is standing behind her; a bloke. Pretty big bloke. Both of them are wearing green scrubs and the woman has her hair tied back tight in a topknot. It gives her face a pinched look, although what do I know? Maybe that's just her regular face. Either way, she doesn't look exactly friendly. Her name tag just says 'Smith'. The bloke's tag reads 'Jones'. If these guys are fake nurses they're not making a real big effort with the names.

'Okay,' I say and head back to the bed.

I sit on top of the bed while 'Smith' checks my pulse and consults a chart on a clipboard. 'Jones' says nothing and does nothing. I glance at him and he looks at me the same way a cat looks at a canary. If this guy's a nurse, I'm a giraffe.

Smith hangs the clipboard back on the end of the bed. 'The police want to speak to you, Theo,' she says. 'Nurse Jones here will stay to, ah, make sure you don't . . . fall over.' Smith glances at the window. 'And no more sight-seeing, okay? Stay in bed like a good boy.'

I nod. What else am I gonna do? Make a run for it? 'Nurse' Jones, standing between me and the door with his hands behind his back, looks like he could snap me in two using his eyelids.

Smith heads out of the ward leaving me and Jones in total silence. It gets real awkward so I close my eyes and pretend I'm sleepy. The problem is, the sedatives the paramedic gave me haven't quite worn off so I actually do fall asleep.

When I wake up, Nurse Jones has gone and there are two men wearing suits sitting one on either side of me. Officer Driver is standing at the end of the bed.

'How you doing?' says one of the men.

'Okay,' I say. 'Thanks for asking.'

He pauses and looks at me thoughtfully. The way he does it reminds me of how Frank Maker looked at me. Which reminds me; no one's mentioned Frank Maker once since I popped back out of his wardrobe in Room 42 at the Iggy. That's weird, right? Not one mention. I file that detail with the humongous stack of details that are piling up in my head. It's a mess in there, I tell you. I have to find a better filing system.

'I'm Detective Black,' the guy giving me the Frank stare says. 'From the Task Force.'

'Uh-huh,' I say. Detective 'Black', hey? I turn to look at the other guy. I'd bet a hundred bucks he's gonna say his name's 'White'. Smith/Jones, Black/White. Like I said, these guys aren't making much of an effort with the fake names.

'This is Detective Honeyman,' says Black.

Okay, maybe I'm getting ahead of myself.

Honeyman bends his head in my direction and does a kind of loose salute with his right index finger. 'Hi, Theo,' he says. A third man, dressed the same as Black and Honeyman (standard issue detective), comes into the room. He winks at me, signals a greeting to the two detectives and pulls Driver to one side. While the new guy and Driver whisper in a corner, Detective Black scoots his chair a little closer to the bed, the rubber stoppers on the legs squeaking on the tiles.

'We got some questions for you, Theo,' he says. 'But before that, I bet you've got a few questions for us. Am I right?'

I shake my head. 'No.'

Black and Honeyman exchange glances. 'No questions?' says Honeyman.

'That's right,' I say. 'But I would like to go home. Right now.'

I'm fighting hard to stop my voice trembling. Not because this whole thing is freaking me right out (although it is totally doing that), and not because I'm not in Bullreedy Hospital like everyone's telling me I am. And it's not even because Driver told me I'd been missing for a year.

No, the reason I'm as twitchy as a frog in a French restaurant is that the third detective who just walked into the room is Frank fricken Maker.

Thirty

When I tell them I'd like to go home it's a bit of a buzz kill. Everyone stops and looks at me. Then Black, Honeyman and Driver all look at Frank Maker to see what he makes of the idea.

He's their boss, I think.

My world somersaults. Maker's their *boss*.

I take a few seconds to try and absorb that information. Two minutes ago, Frank Maker was filed in my internal system as the undisputed Psycho Killer Weirdo King of Scorpion Falls. Now I'm finding out that he's head of this Task Force? The Task Force that's *supposed* to be finding out why kids are disappearing in Scorpi? Kids like me and Lani and whoever else has gone.

'Sure,' says Maker. He looks at me in that creepy calm way he's got. 'No problem, Theo. We're going to sort all this out, okay?'

'Okay,' I say.

'Okay,' says Frank. I'm tempted to say 'okay' one more time just to see how long we can keep it up but the look in Maker's eyes tells me I shouldn't.

'So, you're just going to take me home now?' I say instead and Frank nods. Detective Honeyman goes to say something but Frank Maker holds up a finger and Honeyman shuts up immediately. Maker's got them trained.

'We'll need to speak to you once you've had a chance to catch up with your, ah, mother,' says Maker. 'That's if that's okay with you, Theo?'

'Sure,' I say.

'Dave,' says Maker, looking at Detective Black, 'why don't you organise a ride back home for Mr Sumner?'

Black hesitates for just a second before he recovers. 'Uh, yeah. Will do, chief.' He walks out of the room without saying anything else but I catch him making a tiny shrugging gesture to Honeyman and Driver. None of them are quite sure what's happening. The only person in the room who looks like he's got all the answers is Frank Maker.

'Can I get dressed?' I ask.

Frank Maker gives me a kind of half-smile. 'Course you can, Theo,' he says. 'Can't have you going home in PJs, can we?' He points to one of the bedside cabinets. 'Your clothes are in there,' he says and I think, how does he know that? Maker's right though. There they are; my street clothes, washed and neatly folded, stacked on the bottom shelf of one of the cabinets.

I grab them and gesture towards the bathroom.

'I'll just get dressed,' I say. 'Okay?'

Frank Maker waits a beat or two before answering. I know how he operates now so I wait patiently while he builds the tension. 'Sure thing, Theo,' he says. 'No rush.'

I shuffle past Maker and Driver on my way to the ward bathroom, clutching my clothes close to my chest like a shield. As I close the bathroom door the last thing I notice is Frank Maker holding out his hands, making a tiny 'chill out' gesture to the rest of the men in the room.

I get dressed very quickly and in total silence. Then I turn the tap on the sink full on and look round the room. There's got be a way out somewhere in here and I have to find it in the next thirty seconds. Because the one thing I know for sure is that if I get into a vehicle with Frank and the boys, it won't be taking me home.

Thirty-one

If this was a movie, I'd find a handy window I could get through and that would be that.

Since this isn't a movie there's no handy window. There's no other way out of the bathroom or any magic Room 42 portal I can figure out (although exactly how you locate a magic Room 42 portal, I have no clue).

But there *is* a ceiling made up of square tiles each about a metre wide. I go inside one of the toilet cubicles and lock the door. Hopping quietly onto the rim of the toilet, I scrabble up from there onto the frame of the cubicle which puts me in easy reach of the ceiling tiles.

'You ready, Theo?' says a voice from the other side of the bathroom door.

'One minute,' I answer. I bend down and press the flush on the toilet with my foot, hoping that'll buy me some time.

Balancing carefully on the cubicle frame, I silently push one of the tiles upwards and sideways. The pressed board comes away from its steel mount easily to reveal a dark crawl space between the tiles and the concrete skeleton of the building. I haul myself up as quickly and quietly as possible and lie flat inside the crawl space trying to stay calm. Ahead of me, faint light splinters through a grating sitting across an air vent. I replace the ceiling tile and wriggle across to the vent using my elbows to brace myself against the steel frame. If I put any weight on the tiles themselves, I'd fall straight back into the bathroom. I've just reached the vent when I hear the door to the bathroom open.

'Theo?' Maker's voice is muffled.

He taps a knuckle on the cubicle door. 'You okay?'

I can hear the other men crowding into the bathroom behind him and know I've only got a few seconds.

Holding my breath, I pray the grating across the air vent isn't bolted shut.

It isn't. There are just four plastic clips holding it onto a metal duct. I prise the vent free and wriggle inside the duct. Below I hear the cubicle door being forced open. Finding it empty results in a lot of swearing.

'Quiet,' says Maker.

If I know one thing about old 'Uncle' Frank it's that he isn't stupid. I can almost see him pointing silently towards the ceiling tiles and, sure enough, light floods the crawl space as the cops in the bathroom start lifting them. I replace the vent and wriggle away as quietly and as quickly as I can. After a few metres the vent turns and there in front of me is another grating. This one is bolted shut but it's not strong and I can knock it open with the heel of my hand. I push through the grating and fall about a metre onto a flat roof.

The 'hospital' room I was in must have been on the top floor. I keep my head down and scoot across to a low wall running around the edge of the building. I know the cops won't be following me the way I came — they're all too big to fit through the air vent — but sure as sugar they'll already have figured out where I'll be. I don't have much time. A ladder bolted to the wall leads down to a small yard at the back of the building. Beyond the yard is a path which joins another path close to the perimeter fence. It's only about thirty metres but if I start down the ladder and they spot me before I get to the ground, I'm finished. There's only one smart thing to do. I take off a shoe and drop it over the side of the building close to the ladder.

Then I turn back to the air vent, climb inside and start wriggling my way back to the bathroom. The old switcheroonie. Just like I saw on TV.

Thirty-two

Back down the vent I go, heart hammering, elbows frantically scuffling against the steel. I'm breathing about as well as an eighty-seven-year-old asthmatic. Probably related to all the dust, but more likely to be something to do with the fact I'm dead-set terrified.

I'm gambling everything on Maker and his boys finding the shoe at the foot of the ladder and assuming I've taken off towards the perimeter fence. It's a risk, no doubt about it, but I don't see I've got much of an option. My chances of making it down the ladder had been slim enough. I absolutely didn't have time to get down *and* across the two hundred metres of open ground to the fence. But I'm betting *they* won't figure that out for a few minutes yet. If I'm lucky they'll start searching the area outside the fence. If. If. If.

I reach the crawl space above the bathroom and find the tile above the toilet cubicle. The place looks deserted. That's a good start. I was half-expecting Nurse Jones to be there waiting for me but, nope.

After awkwardly lowering myself back into the

cubicle I tip-toe to the door and press my ear to the wood.

I can't hear anything so I chance opening the door a crack. Just as I'd hoped, the ward room's empty. I take off my other shoe and stow it in a wastebasket. There's no point in leaving it out in the open and it's tricky to walk with only one shoe on. Quickly crossing the wardroom, I reach the far door and look out. There's no one. The nurses have been caught up in the fuss and are elsewhere. I imagine they're involved in the search for me.

A corridor runs along one side of the nursing station. It's empty but it looks a long way before there's an exit out of the corridor if anyone happens to come along. But I don't have the luxury of a choice. I sprint towards a door at the end marked with a bright yellow 'radioactive' warning sign. My logic is that when the search returns to the ward (which I'm sure it will do in about two minutes) Frank Maker might think I'd avoid doors leading to radioactive areas. In normal circumstances he'd be right. But my circumstances aren't in the same postcode as normal.

I reach the door and turn the handle. The thing's heavy but opens easily enough. I'm half-expecting an alarm to sound but it stays quiet. Good. I'd like plenty more quiet happening right now. As the door closes behind me I glance up and notice something I hadn't seen before: a red light blinking above a CCTV camera.

Too late to worry about that.

I close the door behind me and try to get my bearings. Since I'm making this up as I go along — like, what else can I do? — every time I get into a different place I'm starting from scratch. I'm taking every decision now on a second-by-second basis. 'Winging it' doesn't come close.

Judging by the radioactive warning sign, I figure that this door will open into some kind of X-ray laboratory. Instead, I find myself standing on a gantry near the ceiling of a space that looks more like the engine room of a ship. Not that I've ever been on a ship, but if I had, this was what I'd expect the engine room to look like. Pipes run up and down and across every surface while thick black electric cables, bundled together with blue- and yellow-striped tape, are looped along the walls. Everywhere you look there are dials and monitor screens and levers and buttons. But the room's main advantage, its best feature from my point of view, is that whatever this place is, it is completely, wonderfully, empty.

Of course, that doesn't mean it's going to stay that way for long so I need to keep moving, keep dancing. I spot an office chair below with a white jacket draped across the back. The chair faces a high desk littered with papers, two computers and an unidentified bit of machinery. There's also a coffee cup with steam still rising from it. The owner of this desk has only just left.

Beyond the desk is a steel door which looks like it'd be more at home in a bank vault. It might as well have a sign on it saying 'valuable stuff in here'. I'm about to take a closer look when I notice, wedged under the desk, a gym bag. I recoil as I flash back to the gym bag I'd seen back in Frank Maker's room at the Iggy, but a second look tells me that the bag is too small to have, y'know, a *body* in there. I run down the gantry stairs as fast as I can and risk a look. The gym bag contains sports gear.

Including a pair of runners.

They're too small but only by maybe one size. I cram them onto my feet and, tight as they are, I feel a surge of new confidence. Fleeing zombie serial killer psychos — or whatever it is that Maker and his team are — feels *way* worse when you're just wearing socks.

Another glance at the coffee cup. *Tick tick tick*. Think, bro, think! I've got to go, got to get out, got to —

Wait.

Above the desk is a pinboard containing what look like some of the most boring pieces of paper ever seen. Numbers mostly, none of which mean anything to me. But there, half-hidden by a sheet of paper, is a photo. I get closer, lift the paper, and realise I'm looking at a printout of the kids missing from Scorpion Falls. My own face stares back at me from the bottom row: a pic taken at school last year (or was that two years ago?). There's no Corey Briggs in the line-up. And no Lani Lanchester either although I do recognise a couple of the other kids.

And one of them is Ari.

Thirty-three

If someone had run up and Kung Fu-kicked me straight in the face it couldn't have hurt more.

Ari. Oh, man, nononononononono! Not Ari.

My mind racing like an over-revved engine, I take a closer look at the printout. The first thing I notice is that this is not some standard-type flyer handed out across town. You know the kind of thing I mean: a photo of some missing kid with HAVE YOU SEEN THIS CHILD? splashed across it in big type. No, this has the Medullo Industries Research Institute logo in the top right-hand corner. Under each photo are two lines of numbers and letters. I flick to mine and see this on the top line: TS14_(dob12092006)_TayRoScoFa_(dod221220AD). On the second line is this: ClinW2>LABlvl_16b.

I could be guessing most of this — correction, I *am* guessing most of this — but I translate the first line as reading Theo Sumner age 14 (date of birth 12th of September 2006), Taylor Road, Scorpion Falls (date of disappearance 22nd of December 2020). That seems to hang together. With my panic levels rising fast, I see that Ari's date of birth and address are right and her date of disappearance is also 22nd December 2020. The same date as me. One year ago, although that's assuming Driver was telling the truth when he told me I'd been missing for a year. I'm not quite ready to take that as absolute gospel just yet but, for the sake of argument, I'll go with it, which means Ari's been missing as long as me. I quickly scan the remaining photos and all the dates are after the day in the wardrobe. Which makes us the first ones to go. Not Corey Briggs. Not Lani Lanchester. Me and Ari.

The second line of the caption is a little trickier. With a lot of gaps in there I read ClinW2>LABlvl_16b as maybe something like Clinic Ward 2 then the arrow meaning something like 'move to'? If that's right, I'm due to be moved to Laboratory Level 16b.

I stare back at Ari's photo and text. It's almost the same. *ClinW2>LABlvl_16a.*

Ari's somewhere in the Institute. She's here.

Thirty-four

A noise from outside. I scramble frantically behind a cluster of pipes and cabling a millisecond before the door on the gantry opens and two people walk in. Burrowing down as far as humanly possible into the corner shadows I watch a woman wearing a white coat walk along the gantry, closely followed by Detective Honeyman. They're in the middle of a conversation.

'... anything out of the ordinary?' Honeyman finishes his question.

The woman keeps walking. 'Not a thing.' Her movements are smooth and sure as she comes down the steep metal stairs. It's obvious she knows every centimetre of this place. Behind her, Honeyman holds the handrail and steadies himself. Unfamiliar territory for him.

At ground level the woman crosses to the desk and I can see her frown. Something's registered in her subconscious. Some tiny detail on her desk is different. I don't *think* I changed anything apart from taking the running shoes. If she looks in the bag I'm stuffed, but she doesn't. Instead, she stares hard at the papers attached to the pinboard but only for a second or two. With a slight shake of her head, she dismisses the idea that anything has changed and I relax a micro-millimetre.

'How long were you gone?' says Honeyman. He scans the room and I try to make myself even smaller. Honeyman's eyes skate over my hiding place.

The woman lifts her coffee cup and takes a sip. 'Still hot,' she says. 'Honestly, I only stepped out for a few minutes to see what all the commotion was about.'

'Still,' says Honeyman.

The woman shrugs. 'I was hardly out of the room.' She waves a hand. 'And this isn't exactly somewhere he'd stay, right? Most people steer well clear of places with radioactive warning signs.'

'I guess so.' Honeyman's still not convinced. He looks towards the door that reminds me of a bank vault.

'Don't even think about it,' says the woman. She sits down at her desk. 'You need level three clearance to even put in the code. Subject One has no chance of getting through.'

Subject One? Is that me? I think it is. And, if it is me, why have I already got a code name? I only just got here.

Honeyman wanders in a wide circle. He's looking round the room but not paying all that much attention. 'Yeah,' he says, 'you're probably right.'

The woman in the white coat opens a steel cupboard and hauls out a heavy-looking black apron. She puts it on over her shoulders and starts fastening the straps.

'Now,' she says to Honeyman, 'some of us have dangerously radioactive work to do so, unless you want to be fried to a crisp, I suggest you go look for Subject One elsewhere. This place is going to be Chernobyl in two minutes.' I've heard that word before — Chernobyl — but I can't quite remember what it means. It's a place somewhere and I know something bad happened there.

The woman lifts out what looks like a welding mask and slips it onto her head, the visor still flipped up. From a drawer she takes two long black rubber gauntlets and slides her hands into them. Her movements are precise and easy. She's done this before, many times.

'I always wondered what you guys did up here,' says Honeyman.

'We do this,' says the woman.

She presses a couple of buttons on her desk and a hatchway opens up in the wall. Behind the hatch is a steel shelf containing a small wire cage. The woman lifts the cage out and holds it up to the light. Inside is a cute fluffy yellow chick. It makes a *cheep* sound as Honeyman looks at it.

'Aw,' he says. 'Nice.' Then he gets it. Honeyman

stares at the woman. 'Wait,' he says, 'you're not going to?'

The woman puts the chick down on her desk and nods.

'You bet,' she says. 'How else you think we test this stuff?' She makes some adjustments on her computer and the ceiling starts to slide open. In a recess above us is what looks exactly like — and which might quite possibly actually *be* — a massive laser death ray. You know what I mean when I say a massive laser death ray: one of those things evil masterminds have in their volcano hideouts. They use them to shoot down satellites or fry James Bond.

As a powerful mechanism hums into life, the massive laser death ray starts rotating so that its nozzle points down at about forty-five degrees.

The woman in the white coat lifts the cage containing the fluffy chick and puts it on a steel table directly underneath the massive laser death ray.

'I better go,' says Honeyman. 'This seems . . . wrong.'

The woman laughs. 'I thought you blokes in Containment were tough?'

'Yeah, but,' says Honeyman and points to the cage. 'Couldn't you use a rat? I hate rats.'

'We're all out of rats. This was the closest. Just be thankful it wasn't a kitten. Even *I* don't like kitten days.'

Honeyman shakes his head and makes for the door.

'Make sure it's closed tight,' says the woman. 'Once I start this baby up anyone in here will get hit with about fifty *sieverts* of radiation per second.'

'Doesn't sound that bad,' says Honeyman.

'Five is lethal to humans,' says the woman. 'If I was X-raying you for a broken bone you'd probably get 1.5 *millisieverts* per second. And a *millisievert* is a thousand times smaller than a sievert.'

Honeyman can't close the door quick enough.

'Always glad to help,' murmurs the woman to herself. She chuckles softly and turns her attention to the computer.

My hidey-hole behind the pipes suddenly doesn't sound like such a great place to be right now. Fifty sieverts of radiation? And five is lethal? I'm not great at maths but I definitely do not like the sound of those numbers. The caged chick starts chirping and I realise we're in the same situation: the only difference is that my cage is bigger than the bird's.

The woman pushes her chair back from the desk and scoots it across to the metal plinth holding the cage. 'You ready for your shot, sweetie?' she asks the chick in a sing-song voice that makes me want to hurl.

The woman blows it a kiss and wheels back to the desk.

I've got to do something soon or I'm going to be nuked into next Tuesday. At least the woman's still in the room. If I haven't thought of anything clever before she leaves I'll give myself up and take my chances.

The hum from the massive laser death ray ratchets higher and my breathing gets that little bit quicker. I'm fast running out of options. The woman in white checks a couple of monitors and lowers the lights. She moves towards the steel door — the one that looks like it belongs in a bank vault — and presses some buttons on a keypad mounted on the wall. This is it. Time to give myself up. Time to survive.

The steel door slides open and I stand up.

'Hey!' I say and step into view. The noise in the lab is getting louder by the second.

The woman doesn't turn around.

'Hey!' I shout, much louder this time; loud enough to be heard over the increasing drone from the laser death ray thing. Still no response. Too late I see the noise protectors clamped tight over the woman's ears. She steps through the door and it begins to close.

I run. It's only ten metres or so but the door clamps shut faster than I'd have believed possible.

I bang on the metal, screaming. 'STOP! STOP! THERE'S SOMEONE IN HERE!'

The death ray is vibrating fast now and I look up towards the gantry. The other door! Sprinting like a maniac for the stairs, I clatter up them as fast as I can go, praying that Honeyman hasn't locked that door. One level, two levels and now I'm there on the gantry. I hurl myself at the door and grab the handle.

It's locked. Of course it's locked. They're burning cute little chicks to a crisp inside here using freaking massive laser death rays! Of course they're gonna keep the door locked.

The laser death ray reaches maximum volume and a piercing blue-white light cuts through the darkened lab and encases the caged bird. In helpless horror I watch the bird freeze in the light, disintegrating into a shimmer of pure energy before fizzling away in a cloud of sparks.

FIFTY SIEVERTS! FIFTY SIEVERTS! FIFTY SIEVERTS!

The words flash in front of me as the entire lab suddenly vibrates with a blinding, strobing, blue-white pulse of pure energy. Radiation pours through me like water through a sieve — every particle of me untethered from its neighbours — and I become just a loose collection of trillions upon trillions of individual atoms.

For a splinter of time I see and know *everything*. And, by 'everything', I mean *everything*. The entire universe is laid out in front of me in absolutely complete detail. I'm a details guy, remember? Well now I have all the detail I could possibly wish for. Every single speck of matter, every moment in time. *Everything*.

I see my mum, the Scorpion Falls swimming pool, a tiny mole on the side of Ari's face, the maintenance room at school, the inside of a ping pong ball, electric blue graffiti painted across a wall, the Mona Lisa, the roar of the crowd at the MCG, the surface of Saturn's outer moon, a livid scratch on the paintwork of a vintage Bentley parked outside a Bargain Store in an American town I've never been to, the colour of a crocodile's eye as it dips below the surface, a water spout forming off the coast of Venezuela, a happy woman shouting 'Bingo!' at a fairground, an old man stumbling out of a hospital in Reykjavik.

I can taste the tomato sauce on a pie being eaten by a sad-eyed janitor on his lunch break in Katoomba, smell the wet earth after a bad T-storm, feel the texture of a tiger's fur as it stalks an unfortunate and unsuspecting villager in upstate Bengal, hear the squeal of metal from the 12.42 from Lille pulling into the Gare Du Nord in Paris, and taste the salty tang from a bag of hot chips bought from a street cart in Bangkok. I understand everything about quantum physics, know the meaning of life, could perform open heart surgery, and I know what the winning Lotto numbers will be for the next sixteen years. I even understand *algebra*. Like I say, *everything*.

Or maybe not quite everything. There's one thing I don't know. I don't know if I'm about to die or not.

Thirty-five

'Theo?'

The voice comes from somewhere a long way away. Deep underground, maybe. A cave. Or under water. Either way, it barely penetrates my skull, competing as it is with a low background hiss, like static electricity.

The voice again. Louder this time. Clearer. A woman. Mum? 'Theo? You in there?'

I open my eyes. Try to, anyway. It's like trying to prise open a steel trap. When I do get them open, I can't tell if I've succeeded because everything looks just as black as before. For one sickening moment I wonder if I've been buried alive. Maybe I *didn't* die in the lab. Maybe the radiation put me in, I don't know, a coma or something?

'Let's get him out. He can't stay in there forever.' This time it's a man's voice. Harsher, impatient. The sound of knocking: a knuckle on wood. 'Theo!'

This time, no mistake, it's Mum. 'Theo, you've got to come out, hun.'

I clear my throat which sets off a coughing fit.

'Get him out,' says the man and a blinding strip of light opens up in front of me.

'You got any weapons, Theo?' The man's voice is hard, urgent.

'Wha —?' I manage to grunt.

'You armed? A knife? Gun?'

What the hell is he talking about? Armed? Weapons? I want to tell them about the lab, about the freaking radiation. I need treatment. Am I burned?

'Of course he's not armed,' says Mum. I still can't see anything; just blinding white light. 'Look at him.'

'Pull him out,' says the hard voice. A hand reaches through the white light and hauls me up and out of wherever I was. The hand guides me to a sitting position. Something soft, familiar. Blinking furiously, my eyes gradually adjust.

Three faces are looking at me. Mum's in her wheelchair behind two blokes wearing cop uniforms. I'm sitting on a bed in a room I've been in before.

'You been in there long, buddy?' says one of the cops. He jerks a thumb towards where I'd been, towards the darkness. 'Kind of a weird place to hide, ain't it?'

'Hiding?' I say. I follow the cop's thumb.

'We've been looking for you all day, Theo. Turns out you were right here all the time.' The cop shakes his head and points at my hiding place.

It's a wardrobe.

In my bedroom.

Thirty-six

I recognise the cops. One is Tony Clark who I've known for as long as I can remember. The other is Officer Driver.

'What happens now?' says my mum. She rolls across to me, barging Driver out of the way, and puts a protective arm around me.

'He's got to come with us, Mrs Sumner,' says Clark. 'He's got some questions to answer, I'm afraid.'

'I'm not coming with you,' I say. 'I know all about you.' I point at Driver. 'Everything.'

Driver looked at Clark and shrugs. 'The kid knows everything.'

Tony Clark shakes his head. 'Look, Theo,' he says but I cut across him.

'No, you look,' I shout and get to my feet. Driver steps forward and slams me back down onto the bed with the heel of his hand. He's a big bloke, solid, and I hit the mattress hard. Driver puts a hand on the pistol strapped to his belt and pokes a warning finger in my face.

'I don't want to have to cuff you,' he says, 'but

I will unless you do exactly as you're told. Do we understand one another?'

I turn to Mum. 'This one,' I say, nodding at Driver, 'isn't a cop.'

'No?' says Mum.

'Nah,' I say. 'Check his ID.'

Driver blows out his cheeks, reaches into his pocket and pulls out a wallet. He flips it open and passes it to Mum.

'Looks okay, Theo,' she says.

'It's fake!' My voice is raised and Driver gives me another warning look. Behind him, Tony Clark flips out his ID and also shows it to Mum.

'It's not a fake, Mrs Sumner,' he says and Mum nods.

Clark looks at me sadly. 'You think we need medical?' he says but I realise he's talking to Driver. 'You know, like someone from uh, Mental Health, whatever?'

'I don't need someone from Mental Health!' I say.

'You were hiding in the wardrobe, kid,' says Driver. 'And you don't think I'm a cop. That's not exactly someone who's thinking straight.'

'I saw you in Room 42,' I say. 'Yesterday . . . or last year.'

Clark and Driver exchange glances. 'Which is it?' says Driver. 'Yesterday or last year?'

'I — I don't know,' I say. 'You told me I'd been gone for a year. One of the missing kids! One of the eight!'

Clark steps back and presses a button in his lapel radio. 'Officer Clark. Request medical assistance at Taylor Lane. Address in dispatch history. Mental Health. Juvenile.'

He turns back to me. 'One of the eight? What do you mean, Theo?'

Driver straightens up. 'We better not ask anything more, Tony. Could get tied up in procedures down the line, y'know? Let's let the kid get seen and get him his lawyer otherwise we'll cop it when it comes to court.'

'The missing kids!' I say. 'The Scorpi kids! There were eight of them and then I came back through the wardrobe — not this wardrobe, the one in 42 at the Iggy — and then Driver put me in the ambulance and I went to hospital, only it wasn't the hospital, was it, Driver? And I escaped and got radiated and then, then . . .' I tail off, aware that the three adults are looking at me in absolute horror. I turn to Mum. 'What day is it?'

'Saturday,' she says.

'What year, I mean?'

Mum puts out a hand but I bat it away. 'What year?' I yell.

'It's 2022,' says Mum gently.

'Not 2023?' I say and Mum shakes her head.

'What about the missing eight kids?' I say.

Driver steps forward. 'There's only one kid missing, Theo. And that's Ari Patel. As you know.'

'Ari?' I say. 'Only Ari?'

Tony Clark bends down, squatting. 'Are you telling us there are more, Theo?' he says, the colour drained from his face. 'Are any of them here? In the house, I mean?'

'Oh, Theo,' says Mum. 'What *have* you done?'

Thirty-seven

Okay, I admit, it's entirely possible that, to anyone looking at me, it would be fair to assume, based on what I'm saying and doing, I could definitely appear to be losing my grip on reality. Maybe I do need help. But all I know is I'm *not* imagining this stuff. None of it. I saw and heard and felt it all. Every second of it, no matter how strange.

But *knowing* you're not making things up when everyone else thinks you absolutely *are* making things up is *exactly* what someone making things up would probably think.

Which doesn't really get me anywhere except still sitting here in my bedroom being stared at by three people who have clearly decided (Mum included judging by her lack of argument against the idea) that I am indeed a full-blown whacko killer.

While we're all just standing around waiting for the medics or psychiatrists or whatever it is that Clarky had just called in, I take a quick internal run through of the evidence. I mean, I certainly *think* I experienced everything I remembered experiencing right up to and including being fried alive in the secret radioactive lab. But it's fair to say that I don't have a single piece of evidence to back up my story. Not a thing. As far as I can see I don't have any skin burns, which, given the fact I was exposed to enough radiation to melt a cow in two seconds flat, you might have expected to see. I am wearing my usual clothes and — Suddenly, I remember the running shoes! I look down and there's no sign of them. The only thing around my feet are a pair of my daggy white socks. I don't remember taking off the stolen shoes but I guess I must've. There's nothing in my bedroom that I can see or remember keeping: no photo of Lani Lanchester, no photos of the robot spider, no graze on my face where my head got trapped in the lift shaft.

And then I feel it there in the right-hand pocket of my jeans.

Ari's pebble. It's real all right, pressing against my hip bone. I take it out and look at it. It's exactly like I remember: smooth, grey and round. And there, written by Ari, is the word RIGHT! in black marker pen.

'Ha!' I laugh, except it's not really a laugh; more like one of those *'see?'* sort of laughs. I hold out the pebble. Driver and Clarky look at it like it's a bomb.

They're still not getting it so I wave the pebble in front of their faces. 'See?' I say triumphantly. 'I knew I wasn't imagining it!'

'Is that your favourite rock, Theo?' asks Clarky, his voice oozing sincere concern. He's talking to me like I'm standing on top of a cliff and getting closer to the edge. Like I'm a weirdo or something. 'It's a real nice rock, Theo! Does it have a name?'

'Yeah,' I say, 'it's called Eric.' I wiggle the pebble again. 'Of course it doesn't have a name, you dipstick! It's a freaking pebble!' I lean forward and both Driver and Clarky take a half-step backwards, both their hands on the handle of their pistols. Kid or not, they really do think I'm loco so they're not taking any chances.

'The point is,' I say, making sure every word is crystal clear so even idiots like the ones in my room can understand, 'it's the *secret pebble Ari gave me!* She wrote on it! See?'

Driver takes a plastic bag from his pocket and opens it. He holds the bag open. 'Put the stone in the bag, kid. Nice and easy. You say you took that stone from Ariadne Patel?'

'No, I didn't "take" the stone. She gave it to me!'

'Drop it in the bag, Theo,' says Clarky. 'The stone's evidence now, okay?'

'Evidence of what?' I say.

'That you admit to having seen Ariadne Patel and that she gave you this "secret" stone.'

I go to say something but realise that I'm talking nonsense. The stone means something to *me*. It tells *me* I'm not making this stuff up. But to the cops and

Mum it doesn't seem like anything, except that I said I'd got it from Ari. I'm right back where I started, only this time they're all even more convinced I kidnapped my best friend. In the distance I hear sirens and I decide, no matter what happens, I'm not going to get in any so-called ambulance called by Officer Driver again.

I lean forward towards the plastic bag with the pebble in my hand.

'That's the ticket, Theo,' says Driver.

Instead of dropping the pebble I hurl it straight at the window. The glass shatters and, as everyone looks that way, I sprint for the door.

'Get him!' yells Driver but I'm already in the hallway. I drag a bookcase down across the hall, blocking my bedroom door. I zig right into the living room, hurdle the couch and dive straight out of the window, smashing through the flimsy fly screens like they're not there. I land heavily but, as I already knew, it's not a long drop and, crucially, the yard slopes down to our shed where I keep my bike. I drag it out just as Driver comes around the corner of the house.

'Freeze!' he yells and draws his pistol. He's got me but I'm in no mood to stop now. I leap onto the bike and push off down the hill towards the stormwater drain that runs across the back of the house. Two metres, three, four and, with every push on the pedals, I keep expecting a bullet between the shoulder blades.

'STOP!' Driver screams but still doesn't pull the trigger. I risk a glance backwards and it's clear that Driver could take me down with one shot if he chose to. The fact is though, he's *not* doing it. Clarky arrives behind Driver and pulls *his* gun.

'Theo!' he yells and shoots.

The bullet splinters a tree branch about two centimetres from my head but I get round the corner and catch air all the way down to the storm drain, trying not to think about Clarky shooting at me. I land heavy but on two wheels. The bike skids and I wrestle it back under control, stand up and hit the pedals as hard as I can. Another look over my shoulder and I glimpse Driver and Clark running after me.

And, behind them, my disabled mother is sprinting like she's in the Olympic final.

It's the last thing I see before the stormwater tunnel swallows me up.

Thirty-eight

Keep going, Sumner. If you stop, you're gonna have to think about all this.

So I don't stop. Not yet. Anything's better than trying to make sense of what's going on. I keep going. As fast as I possibly can.

I know every metre of the storm drains that crisscross Scorpion Falls. They're bone dry almost all the time, although since we've had rain recently there are still plenty of spots that have a shallow trickle lying at the bottom.

I head east across town towards the Oval. When I can't use the storm drains I try and keep out of sight as much as possible. I can't trust anyone and I don't know who's out there looking for me. The cops? The real ones or the Medullo Industries fakes? Frank Maker?

I heard a thing somewhere once. Something like 'just because I'm paranoid doesn't mean they're not out to get me'. That about sums it up: everyone *is* out to get me.

At the back of the Oval is a skatepark no one ever

uses. It was put in by a bunch of people who didn't know exactly what a skatepark was. Which meant we ended up with a big area of wonky concrete that's falling apart. There's a shade roof behind the abandoned skatepark and that's where I head to try and get my act together. I'm feeling crook but can't tell if that's with, y'know, all that's been happening or if it's down to the little matter of me copping a GIANT dose of radiation back at the Institute.

I put my hand out in front of me. It still *looks* like my regular hand. I don't know what I'm expecting exactly, but I'm *definitely* expecting something to show from my time back there in the Death Laser Lab. The chick on the table disintegrated. Not so much as a scorched feather left. And here I am without even a sunburn to show for the experience. It doesn't make any kind of sense. But not much is making any kind of sense right now so I store the radiation information with all the rest.

Thinking about the radiation lab does have one positive result though. It makes me focus.

The lab. The Institute. *Everything's* connecting back to that place. The Institute spreads through Scorpi and me like a tumour. It's where my parents met. Where the wardrobe in Room 42 led to. Where they have the fake hospital and the fake police. And the weird radiation experiments. The robot spider. And it's got one more thing

ClinW2>LABlvl_16a. The text under Ari's picture.
Laboratory level 16A.
 That's where I'll go.
 Ari needs me.

Thirty-nine

'Look, Davo,' sneers Coley Briggs, 'it's Suspension Boy.'

I've been so wrapped up in, like, concentrating on my ABSOLUTELY MASSIVE LIST OF SUPER MASSIVE PROBLEMS that I haven't noticed Briggs and his right-hand crony, Davo Davies, until they're right up in my face.

Great. Another problem joins the list.

Davo pushes a stubby finger into my shoulder. 'What are you doing hanging round here, Sumner?'

Davo Davies is a carbon copy of Coley Briggs. Not tall, but with the kind of squat build that seems to go with most of the bullies at Scorpi High. Don't ask me why that might be; it just is.

I'd like to say I snap back some smart answer to him but the reality is I don't. In true Theo Sumner style, I let my head drop and mumble something. I know how this'll end — with me getting another bashing — so what's the point of pushing their buttons? It'll only mean more pain.

'So?' says Briggs. 'Why are you here, Sumner?'

'Oh,' I say, without thinking, 'I didn't know you wanted an actual answer.'

Briggs turns to Davo. 'This bloke thinks we're dumb.'

'Is that right?' says Davo.

'Told me right to my face. Said I was dumb.'

Briggs looks at me. 'Still think that, Sumner? How about Davo? Think he's dumb too?'

Of course, what I *should* do is just do my old mumble act but something suddenly cracks inside me. Turns out there has been an odd side effect from everything that's been happening to me recently after all. Turns out I've grown a backbone. Maybe that was what the radiation overdose did.

'No,' I say. 'Dumb is too nice a word for it.' I take a step forward and stare right at Briggs as if seeing him for the very first time. 'You're a moron, Briggs. A stone-cold moron. If you were any more stupid you'd be an amoeba. But because you are so incredibly, mind-meltingly dumb, you won't know what an amoeba is.' I jerk a thumb at Davo. 'He's an amoeba. Look on the info as a contribution to your education. You're welcome.'

For a moment Briggs and Davo stare blankly at me. The words I've spoken are so off the charts from their experience of me that it's taking them time to compute. Then the dam breaks and Briggs starts laughing, followed by Davo.

'You believe this?' Briggs says to Davo but now

Davo's laughing so much he can't speak. Which makes Coley Briggs laugh even more.

'Amoeba!' Briggs gasps. 'Amoeba!'

Out of nowhere, Briggsy smacks me across the side of the head. Hard. It really hurts and I stagger a few steps sideways which sets Davo into a fresh fit of hysteria. I can't help remembering it was *me* laughing while getting bashed by Coley Briggs the night he disappeared. Now it's still me being bashed, except this time it's them doing the laughing. Sort of ironic. I'd have tried to explain that to Briggsy but trying to get him to understand irony would be like teaching French to a wombat.

Briggsy hits me again and this time I hit the ground. I manage to get my elbow down first and it jars my shoulder on impact. I can't see any blood but it can't be far away.

Davo has to put his hands on his knees. 'Wait!' he pleads. 'Can't. Breathe.' As if he's trying to think about something else than laughing, Davo gives me a kick in the side. Just to fill in time, you understand. Like adding punctuation to a sentence. I can't breathe properly.

Briggs snorts and tears appear in his eyes. He laughs and coughs at the same time. 'Bro!' he grunts at Davo. 'You're an amoeba who can kick!' Briggs thinks this is genius level banter and, apparently so does Davo. They crack up some more.

Both of them kneel close to me and start punching.

Punching and laughing. Laughing and punching.

'Amoeba!' yells Briggs and there's a crazy light in his eyes, like he's a numbnut, and I see it in Davo's eyes as well.

They're gonna kill me, I think, as the fists steam in *bam bam bam bam*, both of my attackers still laughing hysterically. And still punching. I put out my hands to try and stop them but it's like being caught in a tornado. A laughing tornado. My fingers clutch desperately and I lock a hand on Davo's throat.

'Uh-oh, Davo, he's got you now!' giggles Briggsy.

Davo laughs.

I try to hurt Davo but I'm a fly. A gnat. An insignificant amoeba. A molecule. With sore ribs and grazed elbows and a few lumps on my head. I spit a glob of blood from my mouth and tighten my fingers around Davo's neck. I don't have much strength so I don't know what good it's going to do.

Then a weird thing happens. And I mean *weird*, even by the recent high standards of Scorpion Falls weirdness. Properly, properly, A-grade weird.

Just for a split second, a moment, my fingers start to *sink* into Davo's skin, as though he is made of butter. It's not a good feeling and I snap my hand back as though Davo is electrified.

Which he might as well be because now Davo jumps up, still laughing but with a kind of puzzled undertone. 'What'd you just do, you *freak*?' he yelps. He rubs his neck and then looks at his hand, giggling as tiny particles drift off his fingertips like dust caught in sunlight.

Coley Briggs stops pounding me and looks at Davo.

'Holy moly, man!' he snorts and points at Davo's neck. 'Look what Sumner did!' There's a clear raw imprint of my fingers on Davo's throat. Briggs laughs like it's the funniest thing he's ever seen. Thing is, Davo does the same, cackling like a madman as he dances around watching those weird particles drift off his fingers. The same particles begin leaking from his throat where my fingers made contact, as though part of Davo is disintegrating. There's no blood, just these strange, shimmering particles.

Coley Briggs lets go of my shirt and gets to his feet. He swallows hard and takes a step away from me. I take a few unsteady steps back, the pain hitting me now the adrenaline from the beating is fading fast. My stomach hurts where Briggsy caught me with his knee. Blood drips from my mouth and I think a tooth has come loose.

Davo's the only one at the skatepark laughing now.

'What did you *do*?' hisses Briggs and I shrug. Because I don't know what I've done, I really don't. I mean, I'm half dead from the beating these two just handed out so I don't even know *if* I did anything, but I do shudder as I remember the sensation of my fingers melting into Davo's skin.

Davo twirls, delighted, hysterical, his arms

extended and fingers trailing pink and white sparkles of light through the air. His neck is *leaking* — that's the only way I can describe it — but still there's no blood, just the release of bits of Davo into the atmosphere.

'This is not happening!' he laughs. 'Sick, man! Sick!'

It *is* sick. It's also impossible. Ridiculous. And completely terrifying.

'Oh Jesus,' whispers Coley Briggs. He sinks to his knees and starts praying. 'Please, God, please save me, please don't let that happen to me, please God . . .'

Davo laughs. 'What are you doing, Briggsy? This is amazing!' Davo throws back his head and twirls and dances, laughing and laughing and laughing as the awful, sickening gap around his throat grows centimetre by centimetre.

'Hahahaha!' Davo screeches. 'Wheeee!'

I back away from him as he spins. Back away as the last scrap of skin holding Davo's head to his body dissolves and, with a soft popping noise, Davo Davies literally laughs his head off.

Forty

I want to be clear about this.

When I say Davo 'laughs his head off', I don't mean that as an expression, or an exaggeration. I mean that Davo Davies has laughed his physical head off right in front of us. As in his actual head is no longer attached to his actual body. Instead, it hovers gently a few centimetres above his neck. Below, the rest of Davo continues to twirl ecstatically, arms extended. It's quite a sight. *Confronting.* That's the right word.

'What?' says Davo. 'What are you looking at?'

Coley Briggs looks like he's about to cry which I'm really annoyed at because that's *exactly* what I want to do and now Briggsy's beaten me to it. We can't *both* start crying. Running was my first option but, once I copped Davo's head floating in space, my legs seem to have turned into two useless lengths of jelly, so that's out of the question. Plus I just got the crap beaten out of me so there's that.

'Aaargh!' wails Briggsy and does start to cry. 'Aaaaaargh!'

'Briggsy, ya big sook!' says Davo's head. Or should

that be plain old 'Davo'? I'm already starting to think of 'the head' as Davo and the rest of him as 'not strictly Davo'.

'Stop crying, Briggsy!' Davo yells. 'It's embarrassing, mate!'

Coley Briggs does stop crying a bit but then immediately starts puking.

'Woah, gross!' says Davo. Which, if you ask me, is a bit rich coming from someone whose head has just detached itself from the rest of his body.

'Do you know what's happened, Davo?' I ask Davo's head. 'I mean, are you aware of what's just happened? Because it doesn't look like you really know what's just happened. And how the hell are you still talking?'

Davo opens his mouth to speak and then stops abruptly. For the first time since his head came off he stops laughing. His eyes swivel south and he disbelievingly watches his own body dancing. I remember reading somewhere about chickens being able to run after they've had their heads cut off. That's what Davo is, I think; another chicken who doesn't know he's done.

'What's that?' Davo says.

'That's — that's you,' I say softly. Bully or not, amoeba or not, Davo Davies just got the biggest shock of his pathetic life. 'Your body, anyway.'

Davo looks again at me and swallows hard. 'My head's not attached to my body, is it, Sumner?'

I shake my head. 'Um, no, I'm afraid it's not, Davo,' I say. 'And I can't work out how your . . . how your head is, ah, y'know, floating? Not to mention how you're still speaking.'

'I don't know, Sumner!' moans Davo. 'I really don't know!' His body stops dancing and stumbles towards a half-pipe. It takes a couple of steps and then falls over, twitching a bit before it stops moving. 'I feel really crook,' says Davo, just before his head falls to the floor and rolls towards Coley Briggs.

Forty-one

'Coley. Coley! Wake up, Coley!'

Coley Briggs' eyes flutter. He moans softly, curled up on the concrete, his knees hugged tight to his chin. He'd passed out cold when Davo's head had rolled towards him.

'Davo . . .' moans Coley. 'He . . . he . . . his head, he, oh, sweet Jesus, Theo! Oh God! That was gross, man, totally gross, right?'

'I'm right here, mate,' says Davo. 'I can totally hear what you're saying!' His head is lying awkwardly on one side, his nose against the concrete.

At the sound of Davo's voice, Coley moans and passes out again.

'You're not helping, Davo!' I say. 'He's in shock.'

'Excuse *me*? I'm like *this* and it's Briggsy who's in shock?'

'Fair point. But him seeing you isn't helping.'

'Could you straighten me up?' says Davo. 'It might help. But cover your fingers with something, okay? There's something wrong with them. It was your fingers that did this.'

'Straighten you up?'

'Put me upright!' growls Davo. 'You can do it, Sumner. You've toughened up.'

To be brutally honest I'd rather drink a rotten rat smoothie than touch Davo's disembodied head. But the bloke's just been — Well, I don't really *know* what's just happened, but it's not good, that's for sure. Compared to having your head separated from your body, it does seem massively wimpy of me not to help him out. I scoot across and pull the sleeves of my hoodie over my hands.

'Careful,' says Davo.

I reach out and, screwing up my face to help stop from puking, quickly set Davo upright on the concrete. There are about forty-six billion questions I want to ask him — *How are you still alive?* being right up there at the top — but it seems kind of rude to ask someone something like that, even when that someone was beating me to a pulp until a couple of minutes ago. I mean, the bloke's just laughed his freaking head off! That's some serious stuff right there.

Besides, there's just something about the situation that makes me kind of *accept* the insanity. Maybe Davo was right saying I'd toughened up. I'd been doing all the wardrobe/Narnia/robot spider/being shot at stuff so it's perhaps not surprising. The thought gives me a little bit of a boost. It feels good.

Coley Briggs is clearly having a harder time making

the adjustment. He wakes up again and starts to faint but the new tough model Theo Sumner isn't letting him get away with that.

'Hey, Coley! Hey!' I bark and kind of slap him across the chops — making sure I cover my skin with my sleeve first. The idea of doing that even a few minutes ago would have been unthinkable, but now I just do it.

You've toughened up, Sumner.

'We've got to help Davo,' I say. 'Understand, Briggs? On account of —'

'You don't have to tell him *why*, Sumner,' says Davo. 'He can *see* why. My head's not attached to my body, you tool!'

It's a solid argument.

'Any great ideas, Coley?' I ask.

'I gotta go home,' wails Briggsy. 'I gotta go. I gotta.' He gets to his feet and starts wandering off.

'Hey!' yells Davo. 'What about me? You can't just leave me here, Briggsy! I need medical attention!'

I can't think of a single medical procedure that would help Davo right now. I'm sure the Bullreedy Hospital hasn't got the capability of re-attaching a complete head. Because no one has. But I don't mention that.

Coley Briggs keeps on going. He shakes his head in answer to Davo. 'Can't do this,' he says. 'Uh-nuh. Just can't, man.'

'*You* can't do this? *You* can't?' Davo's head looks like

it's going to explode. I'm sure if it was still attached to the rest of his body he'd have attacked Briggsy.

I pick up my backpack, open it up and, after carefully making sure my fingers are covered by my sleeves, scoop up Davo's head and put it inside. 'Sorry, man,' I say as I zip him in, 'but this is an emergency.'

'No sweat,' says Davo, his voice muffled. 'Where are we going? The hospital? What about, uh, the rest of me?'

'One thing at a time, Davo.' I put the backpack on and grab my bike. 'Hey, Briggsy! Wait up! I got an idea.'

Forty-two

To say my idea even qualified *as* an idea is probably overstating it. But I flat out can't think of anything else to do so I scoot after Briggs and catch him as he's crossing the Oval. I need time to think, time to be somewhere no one will look for me.

'We have to hide out in your place,' I say. Briggsy reacts like he's about to poop himself. For one scary moment I think he has.

'*My place?* No way! Are you kidding me, Sumner?'

'So what's your plan, Coley?' I say, putting my bike in his path. 'We can't leave Davo at the skatepark.'

'Yes,' says Briggsy, 'yes we can! We can totally leave him there!'

'Thanks a heap, Coley,' says Davo from inside the backpack. 'You know I can hear everything?'

The effect of Davo's voice coming from inside the backpack on Coley Briggs is something to behold.

Briggsy points to the backpack. 'He's in there?' he mouths and I nod.

'And we're all going to hide at your place until we figure out what to do.'

'I'm not figuring anything out!' says Briggsy. 'This isn't my problem!'

'You are such a flog, Briggs,' says Davo through the canvas.

'I don't care!' Briggsy makes to move off so I'm forced to go nuclear. I step in front of him and waggle my fingers in his face.

'Remember what happened when I grabbed Davo?' I say. 'When he was pounding on me?'

'Sorry,' says Davo.

I ignore Davo and get closer to Briggsy. 'If you don't do exactly what I say, Briggs, I'll grab *you* by the throat and *your* head'll come off. Are we clear?'

Briggsy swallows. 'Clear,' he squeaks, in a voice a mouse would be embarrassed about.

'Good,' I say. I step aside. 'Now let's go and see if we can put our heads together and —' I stop and stare at the backpack. 'Sorry, bad choice of words. Let's see if we can come up with something back at your place.'

'I still think hospital is a good choice,' says Davo. 'I vote hospital.'

'We've already been through that,' I say. 'There are a few things about this town you both need to know about. Your only chance is me, Davo.'

Of course, I've no idea if this is true. I haven't got a clue how Davo's head could ever be re-attached to his body. But I do know it isn't gonna happen in the hospital. The answer, I'm sure, like most weirdness in Scorpion Falls, lies inside the walls of the Medullo Industries Research Institute and I'm the only one who knows. If Davo's got any chance — if *Ari's* got any chance come to that — then that'll be where we have to go look.

Just not now. I need to clean up, get some rest. Figure out a way to stop my guts hurting. And my lip. And my head.

If Briggsy's got any more objections to my plan he's not saying. In fact, he's not saying anything. Judging by the look on his face, Coley Briggs may well never speak again. I don't blame him. Apart from anything else I've got his mate's head in my backpack. It's enough to make anyone stay quiet so we walk in silence across the Oval towards the Briggs' house. In all the drama of the past fifteen minutes we've forgotten about one giant potential problem, namely that the headless body of Davo Davies is lying right out in the middle of the Scorpion Falls Skatepark. You wouldn't exactly have to be Sherlock Holmes to get the idea that what you are looking at isn't an accident. It's murder.

With one very strong suspect: me.

Forty-three

Once I do remember about that little detail, the sensible thing would be to return to the skatepark and hide Davo's body. When I say 'sensible' what I mean is 'the least strange thing at the moment'. But I don't go back to the skatepark and hide Davo's body. Mainly because (a) I just copped a hammering, (b) I'm completely freaked out by everything and (c) I just can't face going outside right now on my own. Briggsy's not going to be any use to anyone. It's all he can do to stop crying. He's sitting on the far side of his bedroom sucking his thumb. I think he might have PTSD or something. Again: can't blame him.

Davo is a head sitting up on a shelf so he's not going to be much help. Briggsy's got heaps of movie action figures and Halloween monster masks and horror-type stuff all over his room so Davo blends right in. Unless he's speaking, it's easy to forget he's up there.

Fortunately for us there's no one else in the house just yet. Briggs' mum and dad are still out at work and Nathan, Coley's older brother, isn't back from school. We've got a couple of hours to figure out a plan. If we can. Which is not a certainty.

I clean myself up in Briggsy's bathroom as best I can and swallow a couple of painkillers I find in the cabinet. I've got like a zillion cuts and bruises, a headache that could kill an elephant, and I really should get my ribs checked out because they are starting to *properly* hurt, but there's no time. I'll just have to suck it up. Maybe I am getting tougher, I don't know.

Back in Briggsy's room, I limp back and forth and lay the whole thing out on the line for them, right from the start; right from when Frank Maker walked into the reception at the Iggy and dropped two eyeballs on the counter. When I got to the part about seeing Coley getting into the white van he looks up.

'You remember that?' I say. 'Because when it happened — or just after — you bashed me because you didn't remember being in the van.'

'I sort of remember,' says Briggsy. 'I can remember some creep asking me to get in —'

'That's Frank,' I say. 'Or someone like him.'

'But the next thing I remember is watching the van drive off and you calling me dumb. So, y'know, I figured you probably deserved a bashing.'

'You never said anything to me,' says Davo.

Coley Briggs shrugs. 'I wasn't sure what had happened. It was like I'd skipped some time or something.'

'That's been happening,' I say. 'I think.' I tell them about the missing year and then me getting that missing year back. 'There's all sorts of strange stuff going on with time. And with wardrobes.'

So then I go into the whole wardrobe thing; the one in Room 42 and the lion that turned out to be a lift winch and the robot spider and the fake cops and fake hospital and the radiation room. The whole bit. Neither Davo or Briggsy remembers Lani Lanchester.

'It's a real mess,' I say. 'And Ari's in there somewhere, I know it.'

'Ari?' says Davo. 'The Paki chick?'

'Indian,' I say and give Davo a hard look. 'Are you seriously still bothering being racist when you're just a head?'

'What's that got to do with it?' says Davo.

'I don't know!' There's no reason I suppose why Davo laughing his head off would suddenly make him not be a racist dipstick but I can't help feeling there *should* be.

'I don't like foreigners,' says Davo. 'They look . . . different.'

'Davo,' I say, resisting the urge to throw his stupid racist head straight out of Briggsy's window, 'I don't mean to point out the obvious, but you're not looking exactly *not different*.'

'Why was there no blood?' says Briggsy, pointing at Davo. 'When his head came off?'

'Concentrate, Coley!' I snap. It's a good point about the blood but I can only cope with so many questions at one time. Right now I'm dealing with forming *a plan* and figuring out why Davo's still being such a buttwipe. Plus this headache is getting worse. 'Let's just assume that the no-blood thing has got something to do with what's going on and we'll deal with it later, okay?'

'Just sayin',' says Briggsy. 'S'weird. Maybe . . .'
He trails off. 'Maybe what, Briggsy?' I say.
'Nothin',' he says.
'Tell him,' says Davo.
'Tell me what?' I sit down opposite Briggsy. 'It could be useful, Coley.'
'It's his parents,' says Davo. 'They —'
'Shut up, Davo!' snaps Briggsy. He glares at Davo.
'What about them?' I say.
'He doesn't think they're —'
Before Davo can finish what he's saying we hear a door open and close and the sound of someone coming into the house.

'Coley?' someone shouts in a voice so deep I can feel it through my feet. 'Are you home?'

'*It's my dad!*' mouths Briggsy, his eyes on stalks. 'We're toast!'

Footsteps clump towards Briggsy's room. Both of us turn and stare at Davo. I leap across the room, grab a pair of sunnies lying on the shelf and stick them on Davo. There's also a rubber Frankenstein's

Monster 'wig' which I slam onto the top of Davo's head. 'Don't even blink!' I hiss and hurl myself back across the room just as the door opens.

Forty-four

Coley's dad is a big guy. Like, enormous. Not exactly overweight so much, just *big*. Solid. He looks like the kind of person who could carry a cow under each arm and not break sweat — although exactly *why* anyone would need to be carrying a couple of cows around, I don't know. I try and get my mind to stop thinking about dumb things like people carrying cows and concentrate on looking COMPLETELY INNOCENT. It's not like I've never seen Mr Briggs before, but I've never heard him talk before, never been in his house before and *definitely* have never been trying to hide a disembodied head on a shelf in his son's bedroom before.

'You're home,' says Coley's dad.

'Yeah,' squeaks Briggsy. 'I didn't feel good so came home from school.' Coley's dad turns to look at me. It's not a friendly look but, then again, it's not particularly *unfriendly*. It's the kind of look a great white shark might give a surfer after the shark's just eaten a seal. So, yeah, not a very comfortable look.

'This is, ah, Sumner. Theo,' says Briggsy. 'He's

just come across because I, uh, because I wanted to, um, wanted to show him my . . . um, my collection of, ah, comics on account of the fact that we both like comics, don't we, Theo, hey?'

Too much information, I think. *Shut it, Briggsy*. And, whatever you do, *don't look at the shelf where Davo is.*

Briggsy looks at the shelf where Davo is. And then licks his lips. And swallows hard. Honestly, if he'd been trying to act the part of someone who was guilty about something on the shelf and definitely did not want his dad to look at the shelf, Coley Briggs could not have done a better job. Or worse.

Naturally, Mr Briggs looks at the shelf. Like, gives it a real long, hard stare.

Briggsy and I hold our breath as his eyes travel along, rest briefly on the mask and then — *thank you universe thank you universe thank you universe* — turn back to Briggsy.

'Comics?' says Mr Briggs. 'Do you like comics, Coley? I did not know you liked comics, Coley. Interesting.' Mr Briggs pauses. 'Comics,' he murmurs like he's making a mental note and I see Briggsy looking at me. Davo's words come back to me: *It's his parents. He doesn't think they're —*

Mr Briggs looks at me. He's still standing in the doorway.

'Don't think I've seen you before, Theo Sumner,' he says in a voice that, now it's directed right at me, makes my teeth vibrate.

'No,' I say. I want to say something else but I can't think of a thing. Mr Briggs just looks at me. For ages. Like, it's probably about five seconds, but trust me, when a bloke who looks like he could carry cows under his arm is staring at you for five seconds it feels like a thousand years.

'Okay,' says Mr Briggs. His voice is deeper than the Mariana Trench, yet expressionless. There's so little up and down in it it's hard to tell what mood he's in. He turns back to Briggsy. 'You're usually with Davo.'

Briggsy nods. 'Yeah,' he says. 'Not sure where Davo is.'

Again, Mr Briggs just stands there without saying anything. I reckon we could have been waiting for a year if Mrs Briggs didn't appear in the doorway. As with her husband, I know Mrs Briggs by sight from around Scorpi — at the shops and school and stuff — but have never had any cause until now to be in her company. She's the opposite of Mr Briggs: sharp and small and with quick, nervy movements. Like a rat. Or a bird. Her shiny little eyes remind me of a bird, or possibly a stuffed toy; the kind that has buttons for eyes.

'What are you doing home?' she says to Briggsy, with no trace of warmth. She looks at me before he can reply. 'And who's he?'

'Theo Sumner,' says Mr Briggs. 'He's looking at Coley's comics.'

'Coley doesn't have comics,' says Mrs Briggs. She glares at Briggsy. 'Do you?'

Briggsy coughs. 'Yes, I do,' he manages to say. 'I do have comics. Theo's come to look at them.'

There's a weird vibe about the scene. Weirder than with Davo's head being on the shelf I mean. Like we're all on stage and speaking lines someone's written for us. It feels false.

'Well, we can't stand around all day,' says Mrs Briggs eventually. She and her husband turn away and I breathe a small sigh of relief. It looks like we might have got away with it. If only Briggsy doesn't say something stu —

'How come you're home?' says Briggsy. 'Why aren't you at work?'

Both the Briggs parentals stop dead. They turn back to us and I shoot a small laser glare at Coley. Nice work, Briggsy. I can feel Davo's stare coming at Briggsy through the sunnies.

'We were worried,' says Briggsy's mum.

'Yes,' says Briggsy's dad. 'We were worried.' Both of them look about as worried as a dozing elephant.

'Worried about what?' I say, even though I know I shouldn't.

Mrs Briggs looks at me with her scary shiny horror movie button bird eyes. 'The boy they found,' she says brightly. 'The one with no head out at the skatepark? The police are all there with their flashing lights and tents and all that kind of nonsense. Everyone says it's murder. We thought it might have been you, Coley, because that's where you go sometimes, isn't it, Coley? We were very worried, weren't we, Trevor?'

'Very worried,' says Mr Briggs, flatly. 'Frantic.'

Mrs Briggs smiles thinly. 'But the boy they found with no head isn't Coley, so everything's fine, isn't it? Coley's head is still attached to his body so everything is as it should be.'

'As it should be,' repeats Mr Briggs.

'As it should be,' says Mrs Briggs. The two of them stand there for a few seconds and I wonder if they're waiting for me to chip in with another 'as it should be'. But Mr and Mrs Briggs nod, turn and walk towards the door.

Me and Briggsy watch them leave.

Up on the shelf I notice Davo's sunglasses twitch.

Forty-five

After seeing that weird little parental performance, hiding out at the Briggs place suddenly doesn't seem like such a top idea after all.

As soon as the bedroom door closes, I leap across to Davo and lift off the wig and sunnies. Davo sneezes.

'Man!' he says, snuffling. 'I thought they'd never go!'

I turn to Briggsy. 'What did Davo mean when he said that stuff about your parents? He said something like: *It's his parents. He doesn't think they're* . . . what, Briggsy? What don't you think?'

Briggsy sits real quiet for a while. Then, like he's come to some kind of decision, he reaches under the bed and pulls out a shoebox. Briggsy lifts the lid and I can see it's stuffed with all kinds of junk. I lean closer and Briggsy pulls out a photo which he passes over to me.

It's a photo of the Briggs family from a few years ago. They're all in the garden smiling at the camera. Coley and Nathan are only little, maybe five or six years old. It's a nice photo from before Coley became one of Scorpion Falls' top bullies. It's a sunny day and there's a paddling pool in the background. Everything totally normal.

'So?' I shrug. 'Nice picture.'

Briggsy shakes his head and taps a finger on the faces of his parents. '*Look*,' he says. 'Look closer.'

I glance over at Davo and he raises his eyebrows.

Back to the photo. There's not much different about Briggsy's mum and dad that I can see. They look exactly the same. They're laughing and joking for the camera as though someone's told them the funniest joke ever. I still can't figure out what Briggsy's trying to say.

He rummages around inside the shoebox and pulls out a second photo. Briggsy holds this one out to me and jabs a stubby finger at the image. This one is taken maybe two years ago, at the footy. The Briggs brothers are in their uniforms and posing for the camera with Mr and Mrs Briggs standing behind.

'See?' he says and for a moment I think he's about to bash me again.

And then I see what he wants me to see.

In the first photo Mr and Mrs Briggs are laughing. Like, properly laughing, eyes crinkled around the edges and shining, all that kind of thing. They look really happy, full of life, and you can see they really care for the boys. In the second photo, they look like they're trying hard to *seem* like proud parents, but they look distracted. Not *there* somehow.

'The smiles've gone,' I whisper, half to myself, but Briggsy nods. 'They don't look happy in the second one. Or now. Their eyes . . .'

I trail off and Briggsy looks at the photo again. 'There's nothing in their eyes now,' he says. 'You saw it, right?'

I hesitate. 'I guess so. I mean, they did seem strange. A bit off, y'know? But people change all the time, Coley. They were younger in the first photo, they —'

'No!' snaps Briggsy, suddenly looking very much the King of the Bullies again. 'That's not it, Sumner! It's not that they're "older" or "unhappy" or any of that stuff! Jesus!'

'What is it then?' I say, although I've got a strange and unsettling feeling I know what Briggsy's going to say; what his explanation is for the difference in the Briggses.

He comes in close, then glances back at the door and licks his lips.

'Don't you get it? The people out there are not my parents,' he hisses. 'They've been *replaced*.'

Forty-six

As soon as Coley Briggs lays that little number on me, I realise things must've been going loopy in Scorpi for much longer than I'd thought.

'Replaced?' What does that even mean? 'Replaced by what, exactly? Aliens? Zombies?'

'No!' says Briggsy, annoyed I'd even think of something so dumb. 'Why would anyone be replaced by a zombie?'

The way he says it is like what *I've* said is the single most ridiculous thing he's ever heard in his life. As if everything that's been happening isn't already weird enough. Would zombies or aliens be such a strange thing right now?

'*Replicas*,' Briggsy hisses. 'They've been replaced by replicas. A copy of themselves!'

I don't point out to Briggsy that that's what a replica is: a copy of something. Or, in this case, someone. But, like I say, I don't point that out to Briggsy because it's not important.

'When did this, uh, happen?'

'Two years ago,' says Davo, startling me because

I've kind of forgotten he is in the room. Being a head on a shelf will do that, I guess. 'That's when we reckon.'

'Yeah,' says Briggsy. 'About two years ago. Not long before that second photo was taken. I came home from school one day and there they were. The same but not the same.'

'Did you tell them? Say anything? I'm guessing not because they haven't, y'know, like eaten your brains or anything yet.'

'I keep telling you they're not fricken zombies, Sumner!'

'Replicas then. And there's nothing to say replicas can't eat your brains, just like zombies.'

'True,' says Davo. 'But they haven't.'

It's a good point. Davo seems to be getting a bit smarter now he is disconnected from his body.

'Does Nathan know?' I ask Briggsy. He nods. Then I think of something else. 'Do your parents — the, uh, replicas — know you know?'

'I don't know,' says Briggsy. 'I don't think so. We haven't said anything and they never do anything that makes me think they know. I mean, I guess they could, but I don't reckon they do.'

'They don't know,' says Davo. 'Mine don't, anyhow.'

I spin round to stare at Davo. 'Yours?'

'My parents,' says Davo. 'They're the same. For about the same time.'

'So about two years ago both your parents and Briggsy's got replaced?' I try not to sound sarcastic but I can't help myself. I don't know why I sound sarcastic because it's not that I don't believe Davo and Briggsy. Davo's just a head, right? So it's not like stories about parents being replaced is such a big step. But I want to make sure. 'Isn't it possible you're both wrong? Maybe your parents are the same as they've always been but you're both imagining something?' It feels like what I've just said could be an explanation, but it's clear from their expressions that neither Briggsy or Davo think so.

'We're not imagining anything. We *know*, Sumner,' says Briggsy. 'We just *know*.'

'And you do, too,' says Davo. 'Don't you?'

Davo's right. I do know. Everything that's been happening screams at me that Briggsy's right.

'Maybe,' I say. 'Mum's been doing weird stuff lately.'

'Like what?' says Briggsy.

I flash on Mum sprinting across the street. 'Well, she seems to have working legs again,' I say. 'I've seen her running a couple times. That's different.'

Briggsy looks at Davo. 'Anything else?' he says.

'She put the eyeballs in Frank Maker's room at the Iggy. I told you that.'

Davo whistles. A tiny part of me wonders how he's doing that. I mean, where's the air coming from? I shake that thought because it's getting me nowhere.

The bigger, and *way* more urgent question is, what to do next? I mean, c'mon, here's the situation as I see it: I'm hiding out in the bedroom of the biggest bully in Scorpion Falls along with the somehow-still-alive-disembodied head of the *second* biggest bully in Scorpion Falls and they've both just told me their parents have been replaced at some point in the past. And we don't know what they've been replaced *with* but I'm betting it's not good. I think my first guess about flesh-eating aliens or zombies or something is probably on the mark. And the current thinking is that the same thing has happened to my own mum.

So there's *that*.

Then I can add in that I'm radioactive. Or something. And that Ari has been kidnapped and is (I think) being kept somewhere deep under the Medullo Industries Research Institute. Along with Lani Lanchester, who apparently only I remember, being snatched into a maintenance cupboard at Scorpion Falls High. And then disappearing from like, everywhere.

What else?

How about that there are a whole heap of new cops around Scorpi? And there's the mystery of the woman with Principal Kenwright who went into the wardrobe in Room 42 and never came out. Briggsy getting into the white van and reappearing.

And, and, and . . .

It never seems to stop and, to be honest, I am

super tired of the whole mess. In books and movies and stuff there's always some way of knowing what's going on everywhere: like you see something happen and then switch to see what's going on at the cop shop, or out on a boat or whatever. In real life, you've just got to piece things together as best you can from the information you have in front of you. I'm not really explaining this too good but I know this: not knowing what is going on most of the time is *tiring*. Like super, super massively exhausting. I don't think I've slept in what seems like years. It might only be four in the afternoon but I have never felt so tired in my whole life. I *need* to be unconscious and — definitely, absolutely — not thinking about all the fricken mind-bending STUFF going on in Scorpion Falls. But that's not really an option because (a) Ari's still locked up somewhere in the Research Institute and probably being, I dunno, experimented on or something and I need to find her and save her; (b) Briggsy's house is full of zombie replacement parents (or aliens, or both); (c) according to information received from those scary replacement parents, the discovery of Davo Davies' headless corpse at the skatepark means I am now the prime suspect in a murder and need to keep my wits about me; and (d) a SWAT team just came in through Briggsy's window.

Forty-seven

The SWAT team looks exactly like I'd always imagined a SWAT team would look like. There are five of them, all dressed from head-to-toe in black, wearing helmets and bristling with radios, guns, batons, belts and buckles and a heap of other stuff attached to them. Lots of equipment, all of it black. For all I know they've got cans of anti-shark spray on their utility belts. None of them have names anywhere on their uniforms but I do see the Medullo Industries logo stamped into the metal of one of the SWAT team member's guns. So probably not actual cops.

I know you're thinking that I'm being very cool noticing all these details but I'm about as far away from cool as it's possible to be. It's just that for some reason — probably related to being exposed to dangerous levels of radiation — all the STUFF comes streaming into my brain faster than I would've believed possible in a pulsing wave of detail. I'm seeing things quicker, reacting quicker and scarfing down information like a starving man at an All-You-Can-Eat buffet.

'DOWN! DOWN! DOWN!' one of the SWAT team screams and Briggsy dives straight to the floor. Davo, being just a head on a shelf, doesn't do much except blink. I don't think the SWAT team have even noticed him.

The pointy end of a gun is pushed into my face. 'I SAID DOWN!' the owner of the gun yells, waggling his weapon to emphasise the point.

I feel pretty calm. Peaceful even. I shouldn't feel that way, but I do. Perhaps it's being pushed around by these guys so much. Perhaps it's the years of being a punching bag for the likes of Briggsy and Davo. But whatever it is, I like this new feeling. I'm changing.

'No,' I say to the screaming SWAT guy.

'No?' He looks puzzled. I mean, I'm guessing he's puzzled because I can't see his eyes behind the tinted SWAT team goggles he's wearing. 'No one says no.'

'I just did.'

A second SWAT team guy steps over. He's a bit bigger and a lot more aggro. 'GET ON THE FLOOR RIGHT NOW, YOU MONGREL!'

I notice a dab of white and yellow stuff on his uniform. It's mayo off a burger and I get a sudden image in my mind of the SWAT team calling in at Macca's on the Woody Road junction and it strikes me as being something funny.

Me smiling makes the SWAT guy even madder. He's definitely thinking about pulling the trigger. So I reach out and take hold of the muzzle of his gun. I can feel the metal giving way underneath my fingers, just like Davo's neck did, and I realise there's some connection with me being annoyed or attacked that's triggering this. That's why my fingers haven't been sinking into Briggsy's bed or the backpack or any of the other things I've touched since the skatepark. I'm toxic, dangerous even, but only when provoked.

I squeeze the barrel of the gun into a solid mass of metal and let go. All five SWAT team members stare at the gun like it's going to start speaking. Given what's been happening, that wouldn't surprise me one little bit, but it doesn't.

There's a sort of pause in the proceedings while we all just have a bit of a think about what's just happened. It's a long pause, long enough for me to remember something.

It happened ages ago. Back when I first met Ari. We were at primary school then and she'd just arrived in Scorpi. I guess because I was getting bullied and she was new, we started hanging out. I've forgotten most of that time but now, sitting on Briggsy's bed while the SWAT team is still in a bit of shock about my gun-melting capabilities, an incident comes back to me.

It was break time at school on that first day and I'd been watching Ari get teased by a bunch of other girls. She was new and looked different. They said things about Ari that made me mad; that she didn't belong there, that she was dirty, she was foreign, she ate weird food, the whole bit. Ari was upset and she started crying.

I didn't stick up for her, didn't run over and say something like I should have. The shame of it washes over me even now, even under these circumstances. She was upset and I just stood there. When I knew her better, when we became proper friends, I did stick up for her, but right then, right at the time when she was maybe at her weakest, when Ari really *needed* a friend, I wasn't there for her.

But that isn't why I'm remembering that day. It wasn't what happened (or didn't happen) at school, it was something that happened later on my way home. Something I've forgotten about until now. I'd been walking along thinking about what I *should* have done, replaying the bullying over and over in my head — only this time with me stepping in and helping Ari and being all heroic — when I reached the corner of the street. I felt sick about not doing something and, in anger, I punched a metal pole holding a road sign.

The pole had buckled when my knuckles connected. Like it had properly bent but my hand didn't feel a thing. At the time, I'd put it down to maybe the pole being weak or defective or something because I'd hadn't connected the dots until now. And here's the thing. I suddenly realise that I hadn't got these weird 'powers' in the laboratory. *They'd been there all the time.*

Forty-eight

They'd been there all the time.

The idea rushes through me like caffeine. I'd always known I was different . . . just not different in the way I'd imagined. I'd been able to bend a solid pole. And now I could part flesh, melt steel with my fingers. It's like discovering I was Superman.

Except I know instinctively that whatever 'this' is it doesn't mean I'm Superman. I can't fly or see through walls or make myself invisible or any of those things. I couldn't stop a moving train with my outstretched arm or catch falling planes. I know that without even being tempted to try, in the same way I know I have two eyes, or that I don't like Vegemite. I just have weird fingers that, when I get annoyed, can do strange things.

None of which helps me much with the fact that there's still a SWAT team staring at me and holding at least three more fully-functioning machine guns. They won't be standing around forever. I've got to do something right now unless I want a one-way trip to either the police station or the CI Research Institute laboratory. Neither option is a good one. The cops think I've done something very bad to Davo (which is sort of half true, I suppose, just not in the way they think) and the people at the Research lab — well, who knows what those guys are up to?

Like I say, not good options.

'C'mon, kid,' says one of the SWAT team. 'Let's go. No more funny business.' His voice is a little softer now, I notice. I'm not saying they're actually scared of me or anything like that, but after the muzzle-melting stunt they're definitely keeping a few steps back from my hands. Obviously they could just shoot me, but I don't think they want to. There's information I've got, or something I know, that someone wants. I'm not exactly sure what that is but I'm going to gamble that it gives me a bit of wiggle room in this situation.

Up on the shelf, Davo still hasn't moved a muscle. I glance at him without tipping the cops (if they are cops) off. Davo's eyes flick to his left and I follow his direction.

Davo's looking straight at Briggsy's wardrobe.

It's got one door open.

Forty-nine

It's a big risk.

The chances of Briggsy's wardrobe being another one of those portal things is pretty remote. But there was a portal in Room 42 at the Iggy, I tell myself. And another one in my bedroom back home. Maybe *all* the wardrobes in Scorpion Falls have portals, like they come as standard.

Or it might just be a wardrobe.

In which case, my plans to dive headlong straight through the open door and out the other side into who-knows-where, who-knows-when could be a lousy move. Plus Davo might not be 'saying' what I think he is by moving his eyes that way. Could be he's just got a twitch and I'll end up doing an embarrassing face plant straight into the plywood.

Briggsy's being taken out of the bedroom by two of the cops. He looks at me as he goes past and I get a sudden feeling he's going to blab about Davo on the shelf. I'm no fan of Davo — the guy used to bash me almost as much as Briggsy — but I do kind of feel responsible that, thanks to my new found powers, his head is no longer attached to his body. And, while I've no idea what I can do about getting things back to normal in the Davo universe, I want to at least have a try. I shoot a micro glare at Briggsy. *Say nothing.*

Briggsy keeps his mouth shut.

The door to his bedroom opens and I glimpse Mr and Mrs Briggs standing motionless in the middle of the corridor outside. Neither one of them so much as moves a millimetre when the two cops come out with Briggsy between them. If they aren't replacements, or zombies, or whatever, they're doing a pretty good impression.

'Let's go,' says the cop whose gun I'd melted. He licks his lips, still unsure of what it is he's dealing with here.

'Okay,' I say and raise my hands. 'You got me.'

There's a definite loosening of tension in the room.

I get to my feet and flick a last glance at Davo. His eyes flick to the open wardrobe door and I swear I can hear another faint roar from that lion. I know the lion's not really a lion and is just a winch on top of a lift shaft but it still feels like a sign from somewhere. The problem is, there's a cop about ten centimetres away from me and, even though they're panicking slightly about me being radioactive, I don't want to chance getting dragged back. If I'm right about the wardrobe being a way out of Briggsy's bedroom then I'll only get one shot.

'C'mon, kid,' says the other cop. 'Move it.'

I don't think I'm going to make it. I could do with a distraction.

I get one.

On the shelf, Davo must have been reading my mind because, just as the second cop prods me in the back with the muzzle of his gun, Davo opens his mouth wide.

'BOO!' he shouts. Both SWAT cops scream like little babies — just like the cops back in Room 42 when I'd jumped out of the wardrobe.

Half a second later I dive straight into Briggsy's wardrobe.

Fifty

There is a solid wooden backing to the wardrobe but I melt right on through. This time I notice that it feels a bit like jumping into a swimming pool filled with custard. Not that I've ever jumped into a swimming pool filled with custard, but you get the idea. Sort of gooey and sticky and then I'm out the other side and back in the box on top of the lift in the mines again.

I roll across the concrete and look back. There's no sign of the room I've just come from. No doorway, no sound, no SWAT team, not a thing. And the lift looks exactly like the one I ended up on when I first went through the wardrobe in Room 42. I spot the red metal sign: *DUCT 16/03245. Int/Alt reference G2.* Good old *DUCT 16/03245. Int/Alt reference G2!* Seeing the sign is reassuring, especially when I look for the words *Contractor: Mackay Hydraulics for Medullo Industries* and there it is at the bottom of the sign. I know where I am.

It's funny how once you've been somewhere already it gives you confidence the next time. When I'd got through the wardrobe in Room 42 at the Iggy,

I'd been terrified. I didn't know where I was, or how I'd got there. Plus, I thought there was a good chance I'd be eaten by a lion.

Now I'm back, I feel like an expert in travelling through weird portals. And I do have a fairly solid idea about what's waiting for me at the bottom of the lift shaft. I'm not looking forward to any of it — particularly the robot spider — but at least I do know what to expect. Roughly. Given what's been happening recently, there's no way of knowing *anything* anymore.

I do know one thing for sure: I'm here to find Ari Patel and get her away from whatever's going on at the Research Institute. I haven't got anything close to a plan but I know it'll involve putting as many kilometres between us and Scorpion Falls as possible.

When the winch starts, I feel the air being pushed up the shaft as the lift rises. I wait for it to reach the top and stop. The moment it does, I pull open the metal hatch set into the concrete and drop down smoothly onto the top of the lift. This time I don't wait around. Wedging myself into the gap between the edge of the lift roof, I wriggle down and swing into the lift itself. The whole thing takes about twenty seconds from start to finish. I'm *learning*.

The lift's empty. Which is a bonus because I didn't have anything up my sleeve if there had been someone — or something — waiting for me inside.

I press the down button and hope the lift doesn't

stop anywhere else on the way. I've forgotten if it works on some sort of automatic system but I just go with it: what else can I do? While the lift drops, I spend the time trying to come up with a plan. The best I can do is to start at the bottom of the mine and work my way up floor by floor. I don't really know what level the Institute Laboratory is on so it's going to be a case of figuring things out as I go along.

Something presses against my leg inside my pocket. It's the skull-shaped locket Ari had found in Frank Maker's room at the Iggy; the one with the photo of Lani Lanchester. In all the excitement I'd forgotten about it. I put the locket flat on the palm of my left hand and flip open the lid.

Lani's photo's still there. No reason why it shouldn't be, I suppose, but since her image had 'disappeared' from the school photo in Principal Kenwright's office, nothing would surprise me. She looks like I remember her from Scorpi High: serious, sad, and with those dark shadows under her eyes. She's got the face of someone who's seen a lot of things, most of them bad. She reminds me of me. We could be brother and sister. And, like me, she wasn't a loud person as far as I could figure out, wasn't someone who grabbed your attention, but *I* remembered her. Why couldn't anyone else? Ari had said —

A memory hits me like a punch in the face.

Ari.

With Lani.

Fifty-one

I've never heard of her. Never seen her.

That's what Ari had said. She'd been real insistent about it.

I know everyone at school. Maybe not by name or y'know, know them . . . but I can remember who they are and what they look like. Everyone.

I can see us, clear as, in the reception at the Iggy with me spilling my guts to her about everything that had happened. It was right before Ari had written that weird fortune-telling message on the pebble.

I'd accepted what Ari told me. Why wouldn't I? Just another piece of evidence that I'm the only person who'd ever seen or heard of Lani Lanchester. If Ari didn't know who she was, then she hadn't existed.

But here's the thing: I just remembered a day in school about seven or eight months ago. It was a small incident which is why I'd forgotten it. Or pushed it away because I didn't like what it meant.

I'd been going from one class to the next. Ari wasn't in many of my classes but we were in the same one for art so I was looking forward to it. Ari was pretty good at art and I'm not too bad. Anyway, I'm heading down the long, crowded corridor towards the art rooms when I see Ari up ahead. I pick up the pace to catch her up but, before I get to her, she turns right suddenly as though someone had called her name. When I reach the turn she'd taken, I lose sight of her for a moment before I see her through the window of a classroom. The sun is coming hard through the windows on the other side so Ari's in silhouette. I can't make out much detail but I know it's her. She's talking, fast, to someone sitting at a desk — a girl. After a second or two the girl turns her head.

It's Lani.

Fifty-two

Ari knew Lani.

At the time, of course, I didn't think anything of it. I'd just glanced into the classroom and then carried on walking. Two minutes later Ari had showed up in class and I'd forgotten all about seeing her talking to Lani Lanchester. I mean, why would I remember? Like I said, not much to it. And, months and months later when the whole thing with Lani happened, I'd forgotten all about seeing Ari talking to her.

Or maybe I hadn't.

When I'd first told Ari about Lani and the maintenance cupboard thing, there'd been something about her reaction which had niggled away at me, but at the time I'd pushed it away — probably because Ari had kissed me too, which pretty much made me forget about everything. And maybe she'd just forgotten about Lani. That was a possibility. Not a strong one but still a possibility.

The lift reaches the bottom and I stop thinking about Ari and Lani. That will have to wait.

I back against one of the lift walls as the doors

slide open, half-expecting to see *ARACH16* crouching outside. But there's no robo-spider, just the cold dark tunnel and the dim thump of distant machinery.

I take a few steps out of the lift and start walking. There's still no real plan but after what had happened with me melting the gun in Briggsy's bedroom, I'm feeling more confident than the last time I was in the mine. I'm not saying I'd be, y'know, *happy* to see *ARACH16* coming round the corner, but the thought doesn't have the same impact it would've done the first time.

I walk some more and notice a couple of CCTV cameras along the way. They don't look like they're working but I can't tell. I guess if they are I'll find out soon enough.

About three hundred metres from the lift, I see a light approaching. It's one of the automated trucks I'd seen last time. I find a space close to the tunnel wall and wait for it to get closer. When it passes, it's going slow enough for me to haul myself up a short ladder bolted into one side. The ladder leads to a perforated steel gangway running along one side of the truck. I follow the gangway to the end and clamber onto the roof of the truck. There's a space up there with a seat in it — maybe these trucks do sometimes have drivers — and I slide in.

The truck rumbles through tunnel after tunnel until it reaches an enormous cavern hollowed out of the rock. There's more activity in here, mostly from other automated machines, but I spot a few flesh and blood humans wearing hard-hats and hi-vis jackets. Hunkering down, I try and see if there's any information out there that I can use.

The first, and most obvious, thing is that Medullo Industries likes to use a lot of robot type devices. They're everywhere and they're all doing the kind of thing you'd expect machines in mines to do. Not that I have any idea exactly what that is — I'm no expert on mining despite having lived in Scorpion Falls all my life — but these machines look 'real'.

There are a lot of them though. My mind drifts back to the robot spider. Now I think about it, the robot spider was probably some sort of mine security device. An automated security guard who'd never get tired, never need to rest. And I guessed that having legs meant it could deal with tricky terrain, and wouldn't get stuck on inconvenient rocks.

It's just that it all seemed incredibly high-tech for a mining company. Maybe they —

Concentrate, Sumner! It was my good old inner voice again, this time reminding me to, y'know, do something useful instead of daydreaming about robot spiders.

I spot a couple of mine workers heading towards a wide tunnel branching off the main cavern. There's something about the way they're talking which tells me they've finished their shift.

'And if they've finished their shift, they're heading

back home,' I say to myself. 'Follow those guys!'

Taking care not to be seen by any passing robot spider, or any of the other workers, I manage to get to the tunnel just in time to see the two guys I'd been watching enter a yellow metal door set into a wall about sixty metres away. Hoping there isn't going to be any kind of swipe card or security system in place, I sprint to the door and yank on the handle.

It's locked. Of course it is. I don't know why I imagined it wouldn't be but, there you are, I had.

Frustrated, I punch the metal.

And my fist goes straight through.

Fifty-three

I don't know why I haven't thought of it before. I have some sort of X-men type powers which means if I get worked up enough I can totally do crazy stuff like that. I pull back the door like it's an orange peel and step through.

Beyond the door it's a lot quieter and cleaner than back in the mine itself. Over to one side is a bank of lifts that look like they belong in a hotel, not a coal mine. I get closer and press a button to call one of the lifts. It couldn't be that simple, could it?

It is that simple.

After twenty seconds or so a lift arrives and I get in. One of the lifts I'd been in contained a giant robot spider, but this one is completely spider free. The pad next to the doors contains a heap of numbered buttons. For a moment I panic, the numbers all blurring into one big mess. And then I remember the photo of Ari in the radiation lab: *ClinW2>LABlvl_16a*. Laboratory level 16A. Boom.

Sure enough, there it is on the panel. I jab my finger and the lift doors close. *Keep it together, Ari, I'm coming.*

Fifty-four

I get to Level 16A without bumping into any more nasties. There aren't any security issues and I don't need to put my weird radioactive hands through any more doors.

So far, so good.

Now I'm in the Medullo Research Institute building in a long white corridor, just like the one housing the radiation lab a few floors above. As far as I can work out, the mine lifts 'split' into two on their way to the surface. One bank heads for what I imagine is the entrance to the mine, the other ends up below the Institute. And, since Ari is somewhere in the Institute, that's where I'm going to head for. Or at least try. There's not much security around but I put that down to overconfidence. I'd only been able to get in through the wardrobe wormholes after all.

A glowing LED sign tells me Clinic Ward 2 is just up ahead. I hide behind a soft drinks machine in a corner, just kind of scoping the joint out before I do anything. I've no idea what that might be so maybe all this 'scoping' is probably me delaying whatever's coming next. Which, judging from recent experiences in the Institute, won't be anything good.

I'm glad I hesitate because just as I'm about to try and get into Ward 2, an orderly pushing a gurney passes the end of the corridor. I press back into the shadows and watch the orderly through the glass of the dispenser. Whatever's on the gurney is covered by a pale green sheet. I can't see clearly because of the distortion in the glass but just before the orderly goes out of view I see an arm slip out from under the green sheet and dangle. The orderly calmly replaces the arm back under the sheet and then is gone.

I don't wait any more. It could be Ari under that sheet.

As carefully and quietly as I can, I step across to Ward 2 and open the door. It's heavy but thankfully smooth and silent. Once I'm inside I straightaway realise one thing: Ward 2 isn't a hospital ward.

It's a morgue.

Fifty-five

You know? A morgue? *The place where they keep dead people.*

And, according to the photo in the radiation lab, this is where Ari is.

Closing the heavy door behind me I crouch down next to a long workbench covered in smooth white marble. I don't really know why I'm hiding because if there's anyone in this long white room, they've already seen me coming in. Everything in here is gleaming steel, white walls, cold blue light and a deep silence broken only by the faint beeping of electronic machinery. The room is brightly lit but it's about as welcoming as the grave and as terrifying as anywhere I've ever been.

I've never been in a morgue before but I've seen enough TV cop shows and movies to know what one looks like. The row of stainless-steel drawers lining one wall do nothing to change that view. All that's missing are a pathologist and some cops wearing serious expressions.

After a few seconds of crouching behind the long

desk, I force myself to move. *Do something.* If I'm going to find Ari, going to help Ari, I have to keep going.

That idea — 'helping' Ari — is getting less and less likely with every second I'm in this place. Not much that's good happens here.

There are three rows of steel drawers with handles in the centre. Small digital display screens are set into the corner of each door but the information is coded. A line of numbers and a few letters. No names. No descriptions of what's inside, but I'm about as sure as I've ever been about anything that the steel drawers contain dead bodies. Every atom of me is screaming not to look but I know I have to.

I put my hand out and close my fingers around the drawer closest to me.

Here goes.

Leaning way back — y'know, just in case there is some kind of fricken vampire-zombie-type thing inside just itching to spring out and eat someone — I pull open the drawer. It slides back easily on smooth rails. I hold my breath and look down.

Don't be a body. Don't be a body. Don't be a body.

It's a body.

The body is wrapped in a thick grey plastic body bag with a white zip running lengthways and finishing somewhere near the nose. And it is a nose: I can see the shape pushing against the plastic.

I drop the drawer handle like it's molten lava and leap backwards.

I realise that right up to that moment I had really been thinking the drawer would be empty; that it was all just my over-active imagination.

Seeing the body in there brings with it another unwelcome thought. It could be Ari in there. The more I think of it the more certain I am it *will* be. Of course, it could be anyone — Lani Lanchester for example, or some other poor kid who'd gone missing from the streets of Scorpion Falls —but the thought that it's Ari won't stop.

I have to know.

Taking a deep breath, I step forward and look again.

Yup, definitely a body. No change since the last time I looked about three seconds ago.

The material the body bag is made from is like frosted glass. I can make out that whatever's inside is human-shaped but that's about it. I can't make out the skin colour. There's only one option.

I'm going to have to pull the zip open.

The thought makes me gag. I take a step back again. I don't think I can do this. I mean, c'mon — it's a *dead body in there*.

Yeah, but.

You gotta help Ari.

The voice in my head won't let me quit.

You have to.

The voice is right. I step forward again and take hold of the zip. Here goes. Oh God, I hope this isn't too gross. Like all messed up or y'know . . . rotted and all stinky zombie goop and stuff.

The zip won't move using just one hand so I have to grab a piece of the body bag between my thumb and index finger. The movement brings my face a little closer to the body than I'm comfortable with but there's not much I can do about that. I slide the zip open and stare down into the familiar face of the body in the bag.

It's not Ari.

It's me.

Fifty-six

Someone screams horribly, the sound echoing off the unforgiving steel surfaces around the white room.

It takes a few seconds to realise that it's me who's screaming.

No surprise really. Hyperventilating and feeling like my head's gonna explode is a totally appropriate reaction to finding out that the body in the bag is me.

Or something that looks exactly like me.

It helps if I think of the body in the bag as an 'it'.

I don't think anyone outside the white room heard me scream but, to be on the safe side, I slide the steel drawer shut — taking good care not to glance at 'it' — and duck down behind the lab bench with the marble top. Dropping to the floor, I bring my knees up tight against my chest. I'm doing it to make me look small but it's also because I'm more scared right now than I've been at any time since this whole mess started. New scares are coming at me around every corner, but this is a new horror, a fresh, mind-bending level of sheer terror. I try to tell myself I'm sitting on the floor waiting to see if anyone heard me scream but I know the truth. The truth is I don't want to think about . . . about . . . the thing in the drawer.

The thing in the drawer. That's what it is. A thing. A some*thing*. Me, but not me.

I know whatever that is in the steel drawer can't be me because *I'm* me. I'm sitting right here. But it is me in there. I saw it. *I saw it.*

Some time goes past. I don't know exactly how long. But, eventually, I know I've got to do something. I can't just sit here in the morgue forever. Maybe that's how the other me ended up in one of the steel drawers.

Check the other drawers.

I don't know where that comes from. Check the other drawers. Of course. That's the logical thing to do.

Yeah, and also the absolutely most scariest thing to do. Logic sucks sometimes but I haul myself upright anyway and approach the drawers like they're full of explosives. I pull out the drawer next to the one with 'me' inside.

Just like its neighbour, this drawer contains a grey plastic body bag. I reach out and pull down the zip.

The air leaves my lungs but at least I don't scream. It's another me. Identical in every way to the 'me' in the first drawer I opened.

'It's okay, it's okay,' I mutter to myself as I slide the second drawer shut. I move along to the next one and open it.

Same result. I'm looking at the third 'me'.

Are they *all* me? I take a step back and count the drawers. Three rows of ten. Can there possibly be thirty copies of Theo Sumner in here?

I pull open a drawer on the lowest row. Another grey body bag.

Ziiiiip.

Inside the body bag is Lani Lanchester.

Fifty-seven

It shows how bad things have become that my first reaction to seeing Lani in the drawer is relief. At least there's *something* inside this horror room that isn't a copy of me. Plus, seeing Lani means I haven't imagined the whole thing back at Scorpi High. There *had* been a Lani. I *had* seen Lani Lanchester.

The only trouble is she's dead.

Or is she?

The fact is, I've got no way of knowing if the 'copies' (which is how I've begun to think of the bodies in the steel drawers) *are* dead. They aren't breathing, or moving, I could see that. And if someone's not breathing that usually means, y'know, that someone is dead. But Lani didn't *look* totally dead and nor, for that matter, did the copy of me, now I come to think about it. They looked like zombies. Healthy zombies, for sure, but that's what they reminded me of.

I slide open the next drawer and, sure enough, there's another Lani Lanchester. I keep both drawers open and compare the two faces. They're completely identical. I don't mean they look 'about' the same:

they're absolutely perfect copies of each other. I open another drawer and find another Lani. As fast as I can I move along the row.

There are four Lanis and then someone different in the fifth. It's Coley Briggs. Just like with Lani there are four copies of Briggsy.

And then I have a thought. It's a thought that makes me feel sick to the stomach. Here's what it is: if there are four Lani Lanchesters and four Coley Briggses, then it stands to reason there should be four Theo Sumners, right?

I close the Lani and Briggsy drawers and move one row up to 'my row', my heart pounding. With a trembling hand, I reach out and slide the fourth drawer open. I find myself *hoping* that there's another copy of me inside the drawer, but it's empty.

I feel like I've been punched straight in the guts. There was supposed to be another me inside that drawer, I just know it. This whole place is so organised and precise that the empty drawer feels *wrong*. And then the obvious truth hits me. There's a copy of me out there and I've got a sick feeling I know exactly where to find it. It's standing right where I am.

Because the missing Theo Sumner copy is me.

Fifty-eight

I'm a *copy*.

Not an original. Not the one and only Theo Sumner. A *copy*. A fake. A zombie.

Maybe the most frightening thing about the thought is it makes a strange kind of *sense*. I've never felt like I slotted right into, well, anything. Not school, not my family, not even Scorpion Falls. If I'm honest, I've never truly felt right, never felt like 'me'. And that's because there *was* no 'me' in the first place. After all, there are three more zombie versions of me in the steel drawers right here in front of me.

And, if I w —

'You took your time.'

I spin round.

Nobody. The room is empty.

'In here.'

The voice is muffled. I turn back to the steel drawers.

'In *here*. Second row, third along, you dipstick.'

I open the drawer and unzip the grey plastic body bag.

Ari blinks and looks up at me. 'Can you unzip the rest?'

'Uh . . .' I mumble. 'Um.'

'I'm wearing a T-shirt and shorts in case that's what's freaking you out, bro,' says Ari. She sounds exactly like the real Ari Patel. 'I've got clothes on.'

'That's not the thing that's freaking me out,' I reply. 'What's freaking me out is I'm talking to a —'

I break off and take a moment, suck some air down into my lungs. Something occurs to me. Lungs? Do I even *have* lungs? Or blood or bones or any of the usual, y'know, human stuff that's supposed to be inside regular humans.

'What am I talking to?' I say. It comes out angry. 'I mean are you Ari? Or are you a zombie, or a clone or what? Are you gonna rip me into bite-sized chunks if I unzip the bag? You gonna eat me?'

'Just unzip, Sumner. It's me, Ari. And relax, no one's eating anyone.'

I start to pull down the zip and then I stop.

'What are you doing?' says Ari.

I let go of the zip. Take a step back. 'I'm thinking.'

'I already said you'd be fine!' she says. 'C'mon, Theo, I'm dying for a pee!'

'I know you *told* me nothing would happen,' I say. 'I know you *told* me. But I'm taking a moment to work things out.'

'There's nothing to work out!' Ari flaps around inside the body bag like a landed fish. 'Let me out!'

'How did you know to wake up?'

'What?'

I wave a hand at the steel drawers. 'Okay, all the drawers are shut . . . or they were. And all the . . . zombies inside them are asleep or dead or whatever.'

'They're not dead. Or zombies. I'm not a zombie, Theo, you idiot!'

'Whatever. I'm gonna call you zombies if that's okay. You're all lying there like zombies. Not moving or doing anything.'

'So?'

'So you told me to let you out. Why now?'

Ari grunts in frustration. 'What do you mean "why now"? I already told you I need a pee!'

'But you didn't need a pee when I first came in here. You were all just lying there. Like fricken zombies. And why would you need to pee if you're in a steel drawer? I wasn't supposed to be here. If I hadn't come in you wouldn't have been getting up to pee. It doesn't make sense.'

Ari's eyes flick at something past my shoulder. It's only a tiny movement but I turn around to see if I can spot what she's glanced at. It's a tiny black ball high in the corner of the lab.

A camera.

'Someone woke you,' I say. 'Told you to talk to me.'

'Let me out right now!' Ari's shouting, thrashing furiously inside the body bag, her teeth showing white. Sharp. Her voice changes, shifting down a notch into a low angry growl that turns my blood to ice water. 'I swear, Theo, if you don't let me out, I will pull out your eyeba —'

I slide the steel drawer shut, causing the Ari zombie to screech louder. One thing's for sure: whatever's in that body bag ain't the Ari Patel I knew back at the Iggy. The Ari zombie in the drawer bangs against the sides: *Boom! Boom! Boom!* Then more sounds start coming from some of the other steel drawers as more of the zombies wake up and I wonder if the zips on the body bags can be automatically opened.

My answer comes right away as three of the drawers slide open. One's got the Ari zombie, one's a Briggsy zombie and the last one of the zombies is me. Ari's stopped screaming now and, in the silence, I hear the unmistakable sound of the zips on the body bags sliding open. Turns out the zips do have some kind of auto override after all. Sweet. Zombie me sits up and stares at 'real' me blankly.

There's only one thing left to do.

Run.

Fifty-nine

Slamming through the lab door, I skid out into the long white corridor and crash hard into the opposite wall. The last thing I see before the lab door closes behind me are the three zombie clones clambering out of the steel drawers. I don't know for certain if they're coming my way, but that's *totally* what I'm assuming. Every image from every zombie movie and TV show I've ever seen flashes through my mind at full speed. The fact I've got zero evidence that the things in the drawers even *are* zombies is beside the point. Right now, to me, they're zombies, pure and simple. I push off against the wall and scramble for some grip on the polished floor.

Go go go go go go!

I'm up and running. I hang a right, take a left, then another left, sprinting flat out, zigging and zagging, all thoughts of rescuing Ari — or of me doing anything 'useful' down here in the Research Institute — gone in an instant. I saw a TV show a few months back which was saying a scared animal does one of two things: fight or run. I'm way past the fight option. All I want to do is get as far away from whatever's coming after me as fast as possible. As I'm running, I'm flicking through my zombie memory files. As far as I can work out from my extensive TV and movie research, there are two different types of zombies. There's the slow kind who just sort of stumble around, and then there's the really fast, really angry type of zombie who not only wants to eat you, but wants to do it very, very fast and with maximum violence.

I massively hope these zombies are the slow kind.

But I somehow doubt it.

The thought of the fast zombies gives me the encouragement I need to turn on the turbo boosters. You ever want to find out exactly how fast you can run? Just put yourself in a creepy underground research facility and get yourself chased by a pack of bloodthirsty zombies. In no time at all you'll discover *exactly* how fast you can run.

In my case it turns out to be about six thousand kilometres an hour. I slalom around a corner and almost run smack into a security guard.

'Hey!' he shouts but I dodge under his outstretched arm and sprint for another door up ahead.

'Level 17,' I hear the guard shout into his radio mic. 'We got a mover! In pursuit. Send —'

His voice cuts out as the door closes.

The door leads to a concrete stairwell. Up or down?

I choose up and manage two flights before the security guard makes it to the stairwell. I can't hear the zombies but that doesn't mean a thing. For all I know, these are flying zombies.

'He's heading up!' the security guard shouts and I hear his heavy steps moving my way. But he's older and bulkier than me and *he's* not running for his life.

Clattering up three more flights, I select a door at random. There are more noises in the stairwell and I get the idea the guard has found reinforcements. On the other side of the door is another corridor, this time with carpet on the floor and offices on either side. A couple of startled women look up from their computer screens and I see one reach for a phone. On the wall of the corridor a camera swivels in my direction. Things are unravelling fast.

Three guys wearing suits come out of a door down the corridor. Behind them are two more security guards.

'Hey, kid! Stop! We're not going to hurt you!'

Yeah, right. And the moon's made of cheese.

I spin and run in the opposite direction. Take another left. I hear the crackle of radio chatter and somewhere in the building a siren starts wailing. I don't need to guess who they're looking for.

Then, up ahead, out of nowhere.

The zombie kids.

Sixty

Zombie Ari's in the middle with Zombie Me on her right and Zombie Briggsy to her left. They spread themselves across the corridor. No way past.

'It's finished, Theo,' says Ari. 'Let's stop running, hey?' Her voice is back to normal. She sounds just like the real Ari Patel. No growling or frothing or things of that freaky nature. She sounds *nice*. Which might be the weirdest thing of all. Like this is normal and she hasn't just erupted from a steel drawer in the morgue looking like she wanted to rip my arms off.

'Are you talking to me or that . . . thing?' I say, pointing at Zombie Me. Saying it like that makes me sound like I'm playing things super cool but the harsh fact is I'm practically fainting with fear.

'It's okay,' says Zombie Me. 'We'll be okay, Theo.'

'No!' I bark back. 'No, we *won't* be okay, you freak! There's absolutely zero okay about this situation! So don't try and tell me it's okay! And stop calling me Theo. You're not my friend!'

Zombie Ari holds her hands up towards me, palms out, all smiles and sugar.

'And you stop doing that too!' I snap. 'You're not fooling anyone!'

There are sounds behind me. It's the security guards. Now I'm trapped for real. Zombies ahead of me, guards at my back. No handy doors or windows. No escape hatches. Just plain white walls, ceiling and a carpeted corridor floor. The guards keep moving towards me, although, as they get closer, they start to slow down.

They're wary and that thought makes me wonder why. Why are they scared? If I'm just another one off the zombie assembly line, or whatever it is they're doing down here, then shouldn't they just be able to program me or push a button or something? Why all the chasing and running and stuff? For the first time since I'd opened the drawer containing Zombie Me, I feel a flicker of hope.

'There's nowhere left to go,' says Zombie Briggsy. 'You're just the same as us, Sumner.'

'Again,' I say, 'are you talking to me or the Zombie Me? I'm only asking because it's kind of confusing.'

'He's stalling for time,' says one of the guards. 'Let's get this over with and take him back to Level 16. This one's caused us enough problems.'

The guards are all wearing guns on their hips along with various batons and tasers and stuff but I notice none of them have lifted anything out. I get another little flicker. Everyone's backing off from me. And there can only be one reason for that.

They're scared of something.

It can't be me but, since I'm the one in the middle of this corridor, it looks like it *must* be. The thing is *why* would this bunch be scared of me? Like Zombie Ari had said, I was exactly the same as them. And since they — 'they' being Medullo Industries — could seemingly switch Zombie Ari on and off like a laptop, they shouldn't fear me. If I was 'the same' then they'd do it. Which could only mean that I *wasn't* exactly the same as the other zombie clone things. I *should* be, but I wasn't.

My mind drifts back to the radiation laboratory.

If I *am* one of those zombie clone things maybe the only difference is all that freaky stuff with Davo's head back at the skatepark. I'd got angry, touched his neck and it had ended with him laughing his head off. I mean, it wasn't on purpose; it just happened because I have some weird Spider-Man magic inside me.

I decide to test the idea by walking towards the security guards with my right hand held out in front of me.

'Anyone want to shake?' I ask.

The guards start to back off. 'C'mon, fellas,' I say, 'don't be shy!'

One of the guards speaks into her radio. I can't hear what she's saying but I think it could include the words 'backup' and 'quick'.

'No one wants to shake hands?' I say. 'Group hug?'

'C'mon,' Zombie Ari says. 'This is getting embarrassing.'

I turn and walk towards the three zombies. 'You guys want to shake?' I look at Zombie Briggsy. 'How 'bout you, Zombie Briggsy? You remember what happened to Davo? Wasn't that long ago.'

I have no clue if Zombie Briggsy knows what happened but from his reaction it looks like I could be right.

'Uh, nuh,' says Zombie Briggsy.

'Didn't think so,' I say.

So far, my theory's working great. Even though they were chasing me like crazy, now I'm coming back at them, the guards and the zombies are definitely not wanting to get too close. The problem is, that's as far as my thinking gets me. In the movies the hero — which in this case, is me, I guess — always figures something out and it gets them out of trouble. My problem is I've come to the end of my bag of tricks.

Sixty-one

For a time, we stare at each other. The guards on one side, the zombie clones on the other, with me in the middle.

'Well,' I say, eventually, 'this is awkward.'

There's no response other than the guards shifting slightly on the balls of their feet, like they're about to rush me. The three zombies stay quiet. Even Ari.

Then I hear one of the guards take a call over his radio. There's a crackle of static and he mumbles something I can't hear. The guy who takes the call nods to the other two guards and they turn around and walk away. The zombies haven't got any radios but they do the same. I want to make some crack as they go but when I try all that comes out is a pathetic croak.

I should be happy they're leaving me alone but something tells me them leaving is not A Good Thing. None of them look at me as they go. It's like I've disappeared.

'What now?' I say to the empty corridor. 'What else have you got?'

Not a lot.

I take a step forward and stop. Turn around, take a couple of steps that way and then stop.

'It doesn't matter, does it?' I say. For the first time I notice how cold it is in here. Aircon must be blasting because I'm shivering. If I'm honest it might not be the cold that's doing that.

'Hello?'

Silence.

Then, just as I've made my mind up to run — like just *run*, anywhere, any direction and keep on running — I catch a small movement in the corner of my eye.

A white rat scurries nervously along the corridor wall. I don't like rats anyway but seeing one here just looks . . . wrong. The whole place is so antiseptic, so clean, that the rat must mean something. Everything means something in the Institute. The question is what? It just looks like a regular rat.

The rat sees me and stops. Holding his front paws up, he cocks his head to one side while he takes the measure of me. Neither of us fit in here and we both know it. While we're looking at each other, two doors slide open in the white-walled corridor. I hadn't seen them there before but, still, there they are.

The rat runs through the doors and disappears. I'm expecting the doors to close behind the rat but they stay open. *It's an invitation,* I say to myself. When I get to the open doors the rat is waiting, sitting still in the centre of a pristine white lift. It doesn't look even a little worried by me being there.

'So . . .' I say, feeling dumber than usual. 'I just . . . get in?'

The rat doesn't reply.

Probably because it's a freaking rat!

'I'll just get in,' I say and step inside the lift. The rat scratches its nose and the lift doors close. I'm pretty sure the two things aren't connected but I just don't know anymore. I'm not investigating anything now; I'm not a driver now, I'm a passenger. Whatever they're gonna show me, wherever they're taking me, that's what's gonna happen.

The lift heads down.

Sixty-two

It's strange in the lift, just standing there in silence with the rat. Like, I know it's a rat and all but it still doesn't seem *polite* to stay quiet.

After maybe twenty seconds, the lift stops and the doors open onto a corridor exactly the same as the one we've just left. If I hadn't felt the lift move, I'd swear we were in the same place. The rat exits the lift and turns left, with me scurrying after it like an obedient puppy.

The rat's in no hurry but he's still moving pretty quick. At the end of the white corridor, he takes a right, then a left and another left, with the gap between us growing second by second. I break into a gentle jog but still the gap widens.

'Hey! Wait up!'

The rat takes a turn and when I reach the corner he's out of sight. It's a long corridor — like *really* long — with other corridors branching off left and right. I run to the first turn but there's no sign of the rat.

'I thought you wanted to show me something!' I yell. 'What do you want to show me?'

Another corridor and this time there's a set of white stairs. I clatter up them and, you guessed it, end up in another white corridor, then another and another. For a minute or two I race frantically up and down stairs, turning randomly left and right until I haven't a clue where I am. Because these corridors are really *bare*. No signs, no graphics, no windows, no doors, no sound. Just white ceilings, white walls and white floors. It's like being a —

Lab rat.

The thought hits me like a sledgehammer.

They keep rats in laboratories. White rats. To *experiment* on.

In mazes.

Mazes with white walls and ceilings and floors. Mazes that look exactly exactly like where I am now. I realise that this might be what the rat's showing me. As I walk down featureless corridor after featureless corridor, the pieces start clicking into place faster and faster. For the first time in what feels like years, things are beginning to make sense.

I'm a lab rat. This whole place is a maze. Scorpion Falls is a laboratory maze. All of it. A testing ground for whatever they're really doing here at the Medullo Research Institute. The mining is just a cover; something they have to stop anyone looking too closely at all of this . . . whatever 'all of this' is about. I mean, it's a real mine and everything. Medullo Industries *are* actually digging coal out of the ground and most everyone in Scorpi hasn't got a clue what's really going on. The FIFOs are the miners, the truck drivers and the train crews. As far as they're concerned, they work at the Medullo Mines in Scorpion Falls. They believe that because it's true: they do work there. But *meanwhile* there's this whole other thing going on. A whole different festering mess of cruelty and nastiness with us — the lab rats — copping it all. The zombies in the morgue aren't zombies. They're products. *We're* products. Prototypes of some kind of weird bio-tech development, maybe. The Institute is testing us, prodding us, seeing what works and what doesn't, taking kids off the street and then putting them back out again. Messing with our minds, testing our strengths and weaknesses. Monitoring our every move, making adjustments here and there; little tweaks to the test subjects. Seeing how we'll respond to stimulus.

Subject One.

That's what the creepy baby chicken killer woman back in the radiation laboratory had said.

I'm Subject One. Have to be. And maybe it all gets too much for Subject One and Subject One escapes or starts digging round where he's not wanted . . . so cue Frank Maker and the out-of-town cops and everything else. All of it w —

I turn a corner and stop dead in my tracks.

This corridor comes to a dead end. And there, flush against the back wall, is the wardrobe from Room 42 at the Iggy.

Sixty-three

I'm on autopilot.

The way this thing has gone, I know the next move.

The wardrobe is just like it was back in the motel. Kind of cheap-looking, with scuff marks here and there on the doors. I brush my hand up and down the surface of the wood, feeling the flakes of old varnish peel off under my fingertips.

I pull the door open. Here goes nothing.

It's dark inside, and fully pitch black when I close the door behind me. Frank Maker's clothes are still hanging in place and the neutral smell is familiar. I don't mean familiar from when me and Ari were hiding inside; I mean familiar from when I was little. I've smelt these clothes before, had my head buried in fabrics that smelt like these. A quick memory: me crying and my dad holding me close. It's night time and I've woken suddenly.

'Did you have a nightmare, Theo?'

I can hear his ghost voice as clear as anything. A kind voice but with an odd quality to it. Unrushed.

Is that even a word? What I mean is, that my dad sounds like someone who can't be rushed. A calm person. His voice is identical to Frank Maker's.

Because that's who you are, aren't you, Frank? My dad. My *maker*.

It's hard getting past the hanging clothes but there's more to do, more to see before this is finished. And it is getting close to the finish. I can sense it in my brain somewhere. There are things happening in there I don't want to think about; too many hands fiddling around inside. I push on, further back into the wardrobe from Room 42.

There's a light up ahead and when I get closer, I see it's the woman who arrived at Room 42 with Principal Kenwright. She's wearing white protective coveralls and a mask but it's her all right. She's bending over some kind of tech-looking fuse box thing attached to the wardrobe wall.

'What are you doing in here?' I ask her when she looks up but she shakes her head and returns to her task.

'Not now, Theo,' she says. 'I'm busy. But you keep going, hey, hon? Not much further now.'

Behind the back of the wardrobe the lion roars.

'Hello,' I murmur. S'funny, but now that lion sounds like home. I know it's really just a winch but I almost wish it was a lion. I like lions. I had a lion toy when I was small. Leo the Lion. Leo had an ear missing and some of his stitching was unravelling but I loved that lion. I'd forgotten all about Leo until now.

'Go on,' says the woman in the coveralls. 'Keep going, Theo. You'll know what to do.'

I get to the back of the wardrobe and put my cheek against the plywood. It's warm and the vast underground mine system on the other side vibrates against my skin. All those people going about their business not really knowing what's happening right under their noses. A wave of tiredness washes over me. I could stay here like this forever.

'Not now, Theo!' The woman in the coveralls loses patience and shoves me straight through the back of the wardrobe.

Sixty-four

I knew I couldn't trust her.

The plywood parts like water and I land hard on the concrete. Except this time, it's not concrete — it's bare rock. And, unlike the last time I went through the wardrobe in 42, there is light. A faint red glow illuminates a gigantic cavern stretching out in front of me. The whole place reeks of rotten eggs and I remember something from school about how bad sulphur smells. Where I am now feels way deeper than the Medullo Mine. It's hot too. And I no longer feel all warm and fuzzy about being down here. All that Zen crap back there in the wardrobe has flown straight out of the window. All that hippy-dippy nonsense is gone, like, *BOOM*, gone. *This* is the real deal right here. All my theories, all my smart-alecky deductions and stuff gone like snow on a barbecue grill.

'What are the numbers looking like?'

The voice comes from nowhere, echoes around the cavern.

'What?' I say.

'Quick,' says the voice again. 'Numbers?'

'Not great,' says another voice. 'Down eight percent and falling.'

I spin round but there's no one there. Just me and the giant glowing cavern. Somewhere in the background I can hear the noise of a gigantic piece of equipment pumping away. *Ba-boom, Ba-boom, Ba-boom.*

The red light is fading second by second and, up ahead, something drifts softly out of the shadows. Something big, something Not Good, and heading straight towards me. Whatever it is, it takes its own sweet time, clumping step by steady step, each movement shaking the ground under my feet. Everything gets darker, so all I can make out is a shadow, black on black outlined by a dull red glow.

'Jesus,' I mutter and make the sign of the cross. I'm not a believer but Mum went to church now and again. She didn't shove it down my throat but y'know, it's in there. And, believe me, there's no 'thinking' involved with this: one sight of what is in front of me is enough.

The beast — and that's the only word for it — stands tall on two legs. The legs are those of a bull, complete with hooves and a tail which swishes steadily from side to side. The top half of the beast is in the shape of a man. A big man with hands that looked like they'd like nothing better than to mush me into paste.

But the scariest thing about the creature is its head. It's in the form of a bull, with two wickedly sharp horns curving up and out of its lowered brow.

I've seen this thing before. In school. It was the only interesting thing in one of Miss Fitzhenry's colossally boring lessons.

'Minotaur,' I whisper.

Half man, half bull. All hate. A Greek myth, a story. Except here it is, real as cancer, breathing stink right into my face.

The minotaur lowers his bulky head until his nose is a couple of centimetres from my own. He reeks of something rotten, something best left below ground, something decaying, something dead. This creature *is* death, this creature is my death.

As if answering my thoughts, the minotaur roars. It's a sound like nothing I've ever experienced, a bellow from Hell itself, the stinking waves moving into, through and around me like a tidal surge.

This is the end. It has to be.

The minotaur headbutts me to the floor. Dazed, my vision blurred, I am helpless. Towering above me, the minotaur raises a monstrous hoof and stamps down hard on my unprotected skull.

Sixty-five

The pain. Oh, man, oh man, the pain is . . . intense. The universe explodes into a trillion blinding starbursts, each one of which contains its very own universe of separate pain points. My back arches as my body tries to escape the minotaur's hooves but there's nowhere to go except straight *into* the pain.

'*Mum!*' I scream but she's not here. '*Mum! Ari!*'

Ari's not here either. Instead, Principal Kenwright's face appears, looking into my eyes. He's wearing a white mask and shines a piercing light straight into my eyeball. What the hell is *Principal Kenwright* doing here? This is me dying! Actually dying. Can't Kenwright see he's got no freaking business being anywhere near this scene? This is private, personal stuff with no room for a middle-aged educator from Scorpion Falls.

'He's still active,' says Kenwright. 'Distinct ocular movement.' Another face appears. It's the woman from the wardrobe.

'You still with us, Theo?' she says. 'Keep fighting, you hear? Keep fighting, kid.'

'I'm dying!' I scream but she doesn't seem to have heard me. What are they doing to me?

And then I get it. I'm back at the Institute. Back in for a reboot, or a brain cleanse, or whatever it is they're up to. A great helplessness comes over me. Is this what it's going to be like from now on? An endless series of escapes and being re-engineered? Compared to the minotaur, these people are true monsters. And what about my face? The minotaur *stomped* me!

'Five mill of Porophyl,' says Kenwright. 'Let's get him conscious.'

'Hey!' I say, but that's all I manage before the walls close in.

When I wake up and that's not something I thought would happen when I last closed my eyes — things are a lot sharper.

Except the pain. That's gone and the relief is overpowering. So overpowering that I start crying. I'm not ashamed but, once I've started, I can't stop.

'Don't do anything to me,' I ask. 'Please.'

A woman leans over me and wipes my tears with a cool cloth. It takes me a moment to realise it's Mum. She somehow looks simultaneously younger and older than the last time I saw her. Hard to explain but different.

'It's okay, Theo,' she says. She's crying.

'If it's okay,' I croak, 'why are you crying?'

'We were worried, Theo. We've all been worried about you.'

'We? Who's "we"?'

'Me and your dad, Theo. Who else?'

Okay. Let me think about that one for a moment.

'Dad? The dad who legged it to Tassie when I was a bub?'

'Tassie?' says a voice. 'I'm not in Tassie. I'm right here.' Frank Maker looms into view. 'Hello, son.'

Cue another blackout.

This time when I come round, I don't open my eyes right away. Instead, I listen. I can hear people moving about but with everything kept real quiet. In the distance — like, way, *way* off in the distance — I can hear a siren wailing.

'. . . some disorientation is completely normal,' someone says. 'That will fade in time. It's only been a week, remember.'

I risk a peek. At the end of my bed is Kenwright. He's dressed like a doctor and talking with Frank Maker, who isn't looking his best to be honest. I mean, I recognise him as Maker, but the Maker I knew was all sort of self-contained and confident. This guy has a three-day stubble and bags under his eyes you could fit a hippo in. Maker puts his hand on Kenwright's arm.

'Julie and I can't thank you enough,' he says.

'That's no problem, Mike,' Kenwright says and moves off. 'Mike'? What was that about? Maker/Mike takes a seat next to the bed. Inside a few minutes his eyes close and I take my first proper look around. I'd assumed I was on the same ward I'd been in that day I escaped through the roof tiles but this place seems different. Scratch that, it *is* different. There's a lot more equipment in this place for a start. More bleeping monitors and machinery. More staff. Nurses. Orderlies. People moving around. More colour too; some posters on the wall and a big vase of flowers over to the right. There's a big window too, although the glass is frosted and I can't see anything.

They've moved me somewhere new. Things might have got risky at the Institute. Maybe I raised too many red flags in the parts of Scorpi that weren't part of the Institute? Made sense to get me out of there. The question is, where am I now? It isn't Scorpi, that's for sure.

I turn my attention to the bleeping monitors and try to make sense of them, but it's hopeless. And then I catch sight of my reflection in the screen nearest to me. It's a clear reflection and I can see every detail. There are no scars or markings from the stomping the minotaur gave me. Not so much as a scratch. But there is a massive bandage around my head and about twenty monitor wires attached to various parts of me. I've got a drip going in one arm and some tube I don't want to think about disappearing somewhere near my groin area. I'm not at the Institute or anything like that, I realise. I'm in hospital. I catch a glimpse of blue on the edge of the bedsheet. It's ink. Printed on the sheet are the words 'Property of Mater Health, Brisbane. Ward 10'.

Brisbane? I've never been outside Scorpion Falls. And now I'm in Brisbane? There's something else too; a memory of the rego on the white van and repeated on the lockers in the mine. M8ER WD10. *Mater Ward 10*. What the actual?

'Hey, kiddo.'

Maker/Mike has woken up.

'Brisbane?' I say.

Maker/Mike nods. 'Right here in Brissy,' he says. 'Just round the corner from home!'

'Round the corner?' I say. 'Scorpion Falls is about five hours west.'

Maker/Mike looks puzzled. He leans in close. 'Scorpion Falls?' he says. 'What's Scorpion Falls?'

Sixty-six

Medulloblastoma.

Sounds like a Scandinavian thrash metal band, right? As in 'Here's the new track from Medulloblastoma . . . *Everything Stinks!*'

But it's not the name of a band. It's the name of a disease. The name of my disease. That's one of the things Dad explained to me up on the ward. Medulloblastoma is a cancer. Brain cancer to be exact, and I'd had a fair-size lump of it lodged in my brain for a while before Dr Kenwright and his team chopped it out. Yeah, Dr Kenwright and his team, who include Dr Wong (aka 'Wardrobe Woman') and the married anaesthesiologists Dr Kesha and Mina Patel.

Look, I know this might be a lot of information to take in but imagine how *I* feel. I'll try and explain it all but, given I feel like a minotaur just stomped my head in, I'll probably miss heaps out and get everything mixed up. Hey, I'm doing my best here.

So, like I said just a minute ago, the first thing to know is that I've got cancer. Or had it. Maybe I've still got it. I don't know.

I'd been admitted for surgery three days after knocking my head playing soccer at school. The bump didn't cause the cancer, but they found the tumour while I was getting treated in the Emergency Department. Mum and Dad have been taking turns at Mater Hospital since that night. Three days testing and almost a full day in surgery, they told me. A week of recuperation and things are only now starting to come back to me. Not everything, and only bit by bit, but they are coming back.

Second item: Scorpion Falls.

Turns out I've never been there *because Scorpion Falls doesn't exist.*

I didn't take their word for it. I checked on Google Maps first chance I got and the closest thing online to 'Scorpion Falls' is the Scorpion Cheerleading Program at Niagara Falls in Canada — (*'Recreational cheer programs for ages 3 and up!'*) — which is not the same thing at all.

Now, finding out your entire home town doesn't exist is not something I'd recommend. Because the next logical thought is that *you* don't exist. All those memories aren't memories. All those people . . . well some of them are real, but not like I thought they were.

For example: *Frank Maker's my freaking dad, bro!*

It doesn't get any more confronting than that. His real-world name is Mike Sumner, my very real and very here and now dad. I'm glad I'm actually called Theo Sumner. At least that stayed the same.

Scorpion Falls High doesn't exist. There's no Mrs Rumbass. Turns out I do *like* maths. I'm good at it. So they tell me; I haven't put that to the test yet. The psychiatrist who came round told me there'd be plenty of time to rediscover who I am and what I am. She told me it happens sometimes. Medullablastoma affects different patients in different ways. One of hers woke up speaking backwards and thought he was in the year 1888. Yeah, I'll probably need the psychiatrist.

Medullo Industries? Well, that must've been related to the name of my cancer.

The Research Institute? Nah. None of that happened, but I suppose my brain had got something right: I was in a laboratory. I was getting tested. Just not the way I thought.

There'd been no Room 42. No Iguana Motel. No Coley Briggs (although I do know a Josh Cole and Hayden Briggs from school). No wheelchair Mum. No racist Mum either, for that matter. ('What do you mean, "I was a racist"?' Mum had said when I told her.) No headless bullies. No disappearing kids. No robot spiders. No SWAT teams. No clones. No switched parents (Hello, Mr and Mrs Briggs).

There are some details I don't really want to think about too closely. Like the woodchipper sound I heard in the maintenance cupboard when Lani Lanchester disappeared. Pretty sure that might've been me sorta 'hearing' the um . . . bone saw when they started the operation. The eyeballs? Maybe my subconscious trying to tell me Mum was watching out for me. Or that I was scared I'd go blind? Or maybe just some crazy dream detail that meant absolutely nothing.

Lani Lanchester? No idea about that one. Blame the tumour.

Speaking of which . . .

The minotaur. That's about the only thing in this brain explosion which *does* make total sense to me. I'm sure as sure can be that the minotaur was my tumour made into a monster, something for me to fight. And the showdown in the cavern was my 'IT'. You know, THE MOMENT. The moment when it could have gone either way. My toss of a coin.

Live.

Or die.

The 'die' bit had been close. Way too close.

Mum and Dad told me it had been fifty-fifty but, because they *are* my Mum and Dad, I'm pretty sure they sugar-coated that. The truth is it was probably something more like thirty-seventy, or twenty-eighty, with the smaller numbers falling in the 'Theo possibly lives' column. So I'll take fifty-fifty all day long.

They'd followed World War Theo as best they could, Mum and Dad standing uselessly outside the operating theatre and swilling down lousy coffee in the waiting room. Crying and holding each other while the world collapsed around them. Little messages from the front coming in via the nursing staff. The rise and fall of battles won and lost. The sighting of enemy forces. Hopes rising, hopes fading. Dramatic twists and turns. False dawns and sickening losses. The brave little chemicals and shining scalpels fighting on my behalf. The evil infections and sneaky cancer cells plotting, plotting, plotting.

It's real, that place; the cancer battleground. As real as real can be. As real as it ever gets. And World War Theo isn't over. Not quite. The numbers have definitely tipped in my favour, but there'll be other wards, other machines down the line. Sickness and hospitals, hope and crushing disappointment and all that crapola are going to be in my reality for a while yet.

A really long while I hope because, if I'm still getting treatment, that means Theo Sumner is still breathing in and breathing out. Still in the world. Still fighting. I've got a chance. And, when it all shakes out, that's the only thing that counts.

Or maybe not quite the only thing.

The door to the ward opens and someone walks in carrying a paper bag and a dog-eared book.

'What's in the bag?' I ask, sitting up a little straighter and smiling so much it makes the stitches on my skull scar tighten.

'Grapes, you dope. And your favourite book. What else do you bring your boyfriend when he's in hospital?' says Ari, carefully kissing my bandaged head and sitting down on the edge of the bed. She places the book on the bedside table. I can't remember seeing it before. *The Hitchhiker's Guide to the Galaxy* by Douglas Adams. Sounds good. I think Ari can tell I can't remember the book.

'I don't like grapes,' I say.

Ari opens the bag and pops a fat grape into her mouth.

'I do,' she says, smiling while she chews. 'You should get cancer more often.'

There's a long pause while we stare at each other. Ari has dark shadows under her eyes and her lower lip quivers slightly.

'What's the meaning of life?' she says.

'Big question, isn't it?' I reply.

'What's the meaning of life, Theo?' says Ari again, this time more forcefully. A single tear rolls down her cheek.

'Forty-two,' I reply softly, surprising myself.

'Good answer,' says Ari. She looks like she might start crying properly now, but instead we both begin laughing wildly.

We can't stop.

We won't stop.

More great reading from Ford Street Publishing

Rich & Rare

A COLLECTION OF AUSTRALIAN STORIES, POETRY AND ARTWORK

Edited by Paul Collins   Foreword by Sophie Masson

'*An epic book. Highly recommended*' – Margaret Hamilton

'*This anthology is full of sparkling gems of images and stories*' – Children's Books Daily

'*Chocka-block with delightfully tasty reads from a plethora of Australian authors*' – Booksellers of NZ blog

'*This is a book that every Library should buy, and would make an absolutely wonderful gift for the 10-14 year old reader. Highly recommended*' – ReadPlus

'*An exemplary collection on several levels*' – The Sydney Morning Herald

www.fordstreetpublishing.com   **FORD ST**